Holding

Hast

Drawing his gun, edged to the corne around it again at ground level. The two gunmen were still looking at the van.

At that moment a pounding noise came from it. Hutch glanced that way and saw Starsky lying on his back beneath it. The pounding seemed to convince the gunmen that the two legs protruding from beneath the van belonged to a mechanic . . .

Rising to his feet, Hutch put away his gun. When the girl looked at him inquiringly, he said in a low voice, "We wait."

STARSKY & HUTCH

#3
Death Ride

Based upon the teleplay "Death Ride" by
Ed Lasko
adapted by Max Franklin
Based upon the ABC Television Series
STARSKY & HUTCH
Starring David Soul and Paul Michael Glaser
Created by
William Blinn
A Spelling-Goldberg Production

STARSKY & HUTCH
#3
DEATH RIDE

Created by
William Blinn

Based upon the teleplay
"Death Ride" by
Ed Lasko

Adapted by
Max Franklin

Based upon the ABC Television Series
Starring David Soul and
Paul Michael Glaser

A SPELLING—

GOLDBERG

PRODUCTION

BALLANTINE BOOKS • NEW YORK

ISBN 0-345-23921-0-150

Made and printed in Great Britain
by The Anchor Press Ltd
Tiptree, Essex

First Edition: November 1976

STARSKY

&

HUTCH
#3

Chapter I

THE FIRST THING that irritated Gordon (Whitey) Bomosuto that final morning was that he had to make his own breakfast because the housekeeper failed to show up. His wife was home, but she hadn't made his breakfast in ten years.

Practically run the goddamned town, and still have to cook my own breakfast, he fumed to himself as he scorched a couple of eggs.

At fifty-five, Whitey Bomosuto wasn't particularly happy with his lot, despite being rich and powerful. There were drawbacks to being a racket boss. For one thing, you had to keep a constant eye on your underlings for symptoms of ambition—the only person in the organization he could really trust was Harry Kester. For another, he couldn't get into the country club he wanted to join because a few snooty members kept blackballing him as socially unacceptable. But what made him least happy with life was that his wife was rapidly turning into a lush.

The second thing that irritated him that morning was that Dorothy Kester came by right after breakfast to take Phyllis shopping. He had wanted a showdown with his wife about the increase in her drinking, but her shopping date ruined that.

The third thing that irritated him was that a strange chauffeur-bodyguard showed up to take him downtown. When he answered the doorbell, this huge gorilla-like man with an egg-bald head was standing on the front porch, hat in hand.

1

"Yeah?" Bomosuto growled at him.

"I'm Curly Dobbs," the bald man said. "I'm supposed to drive you."

"Where's Rocky?" Bomosuto inquired.

The bald man shrugged. "All I know is Mr. Kester said to pick you up."

"Wait there," Bomosuto said, closed the door in his face, and locked it. You don't survive in the rackets as long as Whitey Bomosuto had by trusting strangers.

He dialed a number, and there was an answer in the middle of the first ring. "Kester," a pleasantly deep male voice said.

"You must of been sitting on the phone," Bomosuto said.

"I was. I figured you'd call when your new chauffeur showed up."

"What's the matter with Rocky?"

"In bed with the flu. Curly's reliable. Showed up from Detroit the other day, looking for a job. Said he used to work for Louie Sera back there. I phoned Louie and he gave him top marks."

"Okay," Bomosuto said. "I just wanted to make sure nobody was trying to pull nothing."

"You're in good hands," Kester assured him. "See you when you get downtown."

Hanging up, Bomosuto put on his suitcoat and hat and reopened the front door. The huge Curly Dobbs was standing there, but now had his hat on.

"Okay," Bomosuto said. "Let's go."

He locked the front door behind him and preceded the big man down the steps to the Lincoln sedan parked at the curb. As they reached it, Curly Dobbs hurried past him to hold open the rear door subserviently. When he climbed in, Bomosuto noted with approval that a *Los Angeles Times* and a *Herald-Examiner* both lay on the back seat. Harry Kester was efficient all right, he thought.

Engrossed in his newspapers, Bomosuto paid no attention to their progress until it occurred to him that they had been driving for some time. It shouldn't have taken more than fifteen minutes to drive from his West Los Angeles home to his downtown office, and he suddenly realized they had been traveling considerably longer than that. Looking up, he caught a glimpse of the ocean beyond some buildings off to their right, and realized they were on the Pacific Coast Highway, heading south toward Long Beach.

"Hey, where the hell you think you're going?" he demanded.

The driver continued on past the row of buildings for about a hundred yards, then pulled onto the shoulder and stopped. They were in a rather sparsely settled area, with cliffs edging the highway to their left and a deserted sand beach to their right. Bomosuto instantly guessed the score, and made a grab for the right-side door handle, meaning to jump out and run.

The door handle had been removed. He swung the other way, but that handle was missing also.

Curly Dobbs shifted into *park* without cutting the engine, swung both knees up on the front seat, crouched there with his forearms resting on the back of the seat, and grinned at Bomosuto. For the first time in the two years since he had been elevated to top spot, the racket boss regretted his decision to go along with tradition in that job and stop carrying a gun.

Twenty years earlier he could have put up a pretty good fight even without a gun, but too many years of rich food and fine wines had thickened his body with fat. His grinning adversary had no fat on him, and outweighed Bomosuto's 180 by at least 60 pounds.

There was nothing he could do but sit there when Dobbs reached out a huge hand to grip his throat. The big man expertly pinched a nerve, and Bomosuto sank into unconsciousness.

When he awakened, he was lying on the lower part of a double bunk with his hands and feet tied. Aside from a slight soreness of throat, he felt all right. By the sound of a powerful engine and the slight side-to-side sway of his bunk, he deduced that he was on a boat and it was underway on the ocean.

He tested his bonds, but quickly decided there was no hope of untying himself. The knots had been tied by an expert. He lay and waited. After what seemed an interminable time, but probably was no more than an hour, the engine sound changed to idling, and his bunk began to rock not only from side to side, but also from head to foot, indicating the boat was being allowed to drift.

There was the sound of someone descending the ladder, then Curly Dobbs came into the cabin, now wearing a turtleneck sweater and a yachting cap.

"Kester will never get away with this," Bomosuto said. "Even from prison the old man can have him rubbed, and he will."

Smiling, Dobbs said, "Harry thinks he'll stay out of it. After all, he plans to retire when he gets out. Why should he care who runs things?"

He started to untie the knots on Bomosuto's ankles.

"He'll care," the racket boss assured him. "I been like a son to Andy Mello. He named me to top spot, and he ain't gonna like this one bit. Harry will go down, and you'll go down with him."

"No way, old man. Harry's too smart. Who's even going to know what happened to you? There's no evidence of a hit. Maybe an eagle swooped down and carried you off."

He was right, Bomosuto realized sickly, suddenly understanding all the irritating things that had happened that morning. The housekeeper had failed to show because Kester had arranged for her not to. Then he had used his wife to get Phyllis out of the house. That left no witnesses to see who had picked him up in the Lincoln.

Dobbs finished untying Bomosuto's ankles and helped him to his feet. Gripping his arm, he steered him topside. The boat they were on was about thirty-five feet, Bomosuto saw when they reached deck.

Glancing in all directions, he could see nothing but water, which meant they were probably at least twenty-five miles out to sea.

Dobbs pushed Bomosuto to a seated position on the deck next to some lengths of steel chain and a coil of wire. When the big man started to wrap one of the lengths of chain about his legs, Bomosuto attempted to hit him with his bound hands. All that got him was a backhand cuff that stunned him enough to allow Dobbs to complete the job in peace. When he became clearheaded again, his body was wrapped in three lengths of heavy chains that had been wired into place.

"Listen, let's make a deal," Bomosuto said. "I'll set you up in Kester's place."

"I ain't the executive type," Dobbs said. "This is the kind of work I do best. It pays good, and I never have to worry about some guy doing it to *me*."

He stooped to pick Bomosuto up in his arms. It took considerable effort, because the chains weighed about fifteen pounds apiece, which made the total load about 225. Grunting under the load, the big man staggered toward the rail.

"Listen," Bomosuto said in a frantic voice.

That was the last thing he ever said, because the big man heaved his chain-wrapped figure over the rail.

Harry Kester deliberately scheduled the meeting in Whitey Bomosuto's office instead of in his own, on the principle that possession is nine points of the law. He figured there was bound to be a certain psychological effect in seeing him seated behind the desk of power.

Kester was a rather small man physically, only five feet six and weighing about 140 pounds. But at thirty-four he was muscled like an athlete, and there was an air of authority about him that brought instant attention when he spoke. He had no difficulty dominating the meeting.

As soon as the last member of the organization

was in the room, he got right to the point. He said, "I called you all together to decide what to do about Whitey disappearing the way he did. We can't run things forever not knowing where the hell he is, or if he's ever coming back. So temporarily, until he does turn up, if he's ever gonna, I'm taking over in his name. Naturally I'll step down again if he does come back, but meantime I'm sitting in this seat. Any objections?"

Jake Timmins, who ran the numbers operation in the downtown section, looked as though he might have an objection, but after thoughtfully examining the bald-headed Curly Dobbs, who stood behind Kester's chair with his arms folded and his teeth showing in a humorless grin, he decided not to voice it. No one else seemed inclined to challenge Kester's assumption of power.

After a seemly wait, Kester said, "I guess there's no objection. Let's have your reports." He looked at Timmins. "Jake, you can start off."

Chapter II

THE PRISONER ESCORTED by the guard into the warden's office of the federal prison was about sixty-five, tall, distinguished-looking, and gray-haired. Despite his prison uniform and his stubbly prison haircut, he somehow managed to look more like a business executive than a convict. His normally expressionless eyes momentarily showed surprise at the well-dressed middle-aged visitor seated in a chair alongside the warden's desk, but then became opaque again. He said nothing, merely coming to a halt before the desk and waiting.

The plump, prematurely gray man seated behind the desk said to the guard, "Okay, Mel, you don't have to wait."

The guard looked slightly surprised, since it was not customary to leave an unattended prisoner with the warden, but he merely said, "Yes, sir," and left.

As soon as the door closed behind the guard, the middle-aged visitor rose to his feet and, smiling broadly, thrust out his hand to the prisoner. "How are you, Andrew?" he asked.

Cordially gripping the hand, Andrew Mello said, "Fine, Wayne. I didn't expect to see you for another week."

The warden said, "Mr. Parks is here to pick you up, Mello. You're leaving today."

Mello glanced at the warden, then back at his attorney. "Oh?"

"Today has been your arranged release date all along," the lawyer explained. "We deliberately announced it as next week for security reasons."

Andrew Mello's eyes narrowed slightly, but again all he said was, "Oh?"

"Not letting you know was Don Coleman's idea, not mine," Wayne Parks said. "He wanted to make absolutely sure there'd be no leak I told him you weren't the sort to sound off to your cellmate, but you know how those guys are."

"What guys? Who the hell is Don Coleman?"

The lawyer looked faintly surprised. "The Los Angeles D.A. I guess you wouldn't know. He's only been in office two years, and you've been here three."

After considering this, Mello said dryly, "I'm touched by his concern, but why do I need security arrangements?"

"Coleman got a tip that there's a contract out on you."

If the news disturbed the older man, it didn't show.

He merely looked thoughtful. After a time he said, "Kester?"

"Who else?"

"Why? I've made it clear enough I've retired."

The lawyer threw a side-glance at the warden. Shrugging, Mello dropped the subject. Turning to the man seated behind the desk, he said, "Do I get a government-issue suit of clothes in exchange for my uniform, warden?"

The warden said, "Mr. Parks thought you would prefer something of better quality. You'll find a suitcase in my private washroom."

Mello threw his lawyer a bleak smile. "You always think of everything, Wayne. I should have let you do my bookkeeping instead of that moronic accountant."

Parks shook his head. "You wouldn't have taken my advice on that, Andrew. I *told* you trying to cheat the IRS was dumb."

"Greed is a terrible sin," Mello admitted sardonically. "But, only if you get caught."

He crossed the office to the washroom door and disappeared through it.

Fifteen minutes later the newly freed prisoner and his lawyer were passed through the main prison gate. Mello now wore an expensive gray pinstripe suit, a white shirt, and a silver-and-black-striped necktie with a ruby stickpin. His short prison haircut was concealed by a pearl-gray homburg. The lawyer was carrying the now empty suitcase.

Parked at the curb directly in front of the main gate was a black limousine. In the front seat sat two men, both in their mid-forties, both wearing neat but inexpensive business suits and alert expressions. The one behind the wheel was heavy-shouldered and thick-waisted, the other was tall and lanky. The latter reached over to remove the keys from the ignition lock, got out of the car, and opened the trunk for Wayne Parks to deposit the suitcase.

After slamming the trunk lid, Parks said to Andrew Mello, "This is Sergeant Darrow of the L.A.P.D.,

Andrew." Then he nodded toward the driver, still seated behind the wheel. "And Officer Phelps."

Mello gave each man a quick nod. Both detectives nodded back, just as quickly. Sergeant Darrow held open the rear door of the limousine for Mello and the lawyer to climb in, then reseated himself in the front seat and handed the keys to the driver. As the car pulled away, Parks leaned forward to slide closed the thick glass pane separating the rear compartment from the front seat.

Glancing at him, Mello asked tonelessly, "Sure it's not bugged?"

"It's not a police vehicle," the lawyer said. "I rented it myself, and those guys were never in it until I picked them up this morning."

The older man nodded approvingly. "You *do* think of everything, Wayne. Now what's this all about?"

"They're your assigned bodyguards."

"I deduced that," Mello said. "Why do I need bodyguards?"

"I told you Kester put out a contract on you."

In a patient tone Mello said, "Don't make me pry it out of you, Wayne. I made it clear to everybody when I went into the joint that I was retiring. I didn't pick *him* to step in my shoes, but I didn't pull any strings to keep him out of them either. So what's his beef?"

"Maybe he resents you turning things over to Whitey instead of to him, Andrew."

Mello made an impatient gesture. "Aw, come on. Whitey'd been my right arm before Kester was even a two-bit bag man. I was sore when I got the news that Whitey'd disappeared, sure, but if I'd been sore enough to do anything about it, I wouldn't have waited until now. Even behind bars I still had enough clout to get Kester canceled if I had wanted to. But I thought, what the hell? What was done, was done; and having Kester hit just for revenge might have wrecked the whole organization. With the top spot up for grabs, even old friends would be gunning each other. Since

I was retiring anyway, I stayed out of it. And I made sure Kester got the word I was staying out."

There was silence for a few moments. The limousine entered a freeway on-ramp, and from the habit of a lifetime of survival training Mello cast a wary eye at the traffic alongside of them until the limousine got out of the acceleration lane. Finally he turned back to the lawyer again and said, "You're trying to break something to me gently, aren't you?"

Parks' gaze briefly touched his face, then shifted away. "I'm not sure you'll like it, Andrew. But it wasn't my doing. All I did was listen to Coleman and agree to pass on to you what he said. We think there was a leak, and what we were talking about got to Kester."

Mello's eyes suddenly developed a strange glitter. "Spill it, Wayne," he said softly. "All of it."

Parks glanced at him again, saw the glitter, and uneasily shifted his gaze away a second time. "We think Kester may have heard you were going to testify against him before the grand jury."

The glitter became brighter and the voice became softer. "Now why would he hear anything like that, Wayne?"

The lawyer took a deep breath, then expelled it before saying, "Let me start at the beginning. The Morgan thing isn't dead, Andrew."

"The hell it isn't. That was buried even before they nailed me for income-tax evasion. You told me so yourself."

Parks shook his head. "It was only tabled for lack of evidence. There's no statute of limitations on conspiracy to commit murder, and Coleman's untabled it. He got Bonnie to talk."

The glitter faded from the older man's eyes and he looked slightly startled.

"Why'd you ever pull a thing like that with a floozy sitting in the car?" the lawyer asked querulously. "She told Coleman how you spotted Morgan on the street, and ordered Whitey to pull over, how Whitey held Morgan around the throat from behind while you questioned him about skimming his numbers collections before turning them in, how you then gave Whitey the nod, climbed back in the car, and how Whitey cut his throat. Coleman's got her in protective custody, and he says she's willing to testify on the stand. He played me the tape of the interview with her, and it's dynamite."

For a long time, Mello eyed the traffic in the lane next to them with a brooding expression on his face, then asked, "No way to get to Bonnie?"

"None. Coeman's got her out of town somewhere, under twenty-four-hour guard."

"Think this Coleman fellow can get a conviction?"

"It looks airtight to me, Andrew."

Mello emitted a sigh. "Okay, I can guess the rest. The D.A. came to you, laid it all out, then offered me a deal if I'd give him Kester. How good a deal?"

"Complete immunity."

Mello pursed his lips in a soundless whistle. "He must want Kester bad."

"As bad as his predecessor wanted you. I didn't promise him a thing. I just said I'd relay the offer to you. He won't play around, though, Andrew. He made it clear that if you won't deal, he's going for Murder One. There's no chance of bargaining to reduce the charge to manslaughter in return for a guilty plea."

"All or nothing, eh?" Mello said musingly. "What kind of bust he want Kester on?"

"Something big. He won't settle for the Mann Act, or dope-dealing, or illegal gambling. He'd like him for murder."

"How the hell could I testify on that?" Mello asked in an irritated voice. "I was in the federal slammer when he had Whitey hit."

The lawyer shrugged. "He's not particular about what murder."

After contemplating, Mello said, "I could give him a half dozen, but not without incriminating myself for ordering them."

"Coleman guaranteed full immunity for everything, not just for Morgan. He wants Kester that bad."

Grunting, Mello went into a gloomy think. Presently he asked, "What's your advice?"

"Testify."

Mello nodded. "It's not as though I'd just be saving my own skin. I got a legitimate gripe against Kester for wasting Whitey."

"Of course you have, Andrew. Besides, he put out a contract on you."

Mello frowned. "How the hell did he find out Coleman was offering a deal?"

The lawyer shrugged again. "There had to be a leak. It wasn't from my office, because I didn't even tell my secretary about the offer."

"From the D.A.'s office, then."

Shaking his head, Parks said, "Not necessarily. Could have been from the police department. Naturally Coleman kept the team that's been investigating Kester informed of his plans."

"What team's that?"

"Couple of Captain Dobey's men, Dave Starsky and Ken Hutchinson."

"They on the take?"

Parks emitted a brief laugh.

"What's so funny?" the older man asked.

"Neither of them's the leak. Take my word for it."

"They something special?"

"Yeah. They're the exception that proves your favorite rule."

"What rule?" Mello asked, frowning.

"That every man has his price. They haven't."

Andrew Mello's lips curled in a sardonic smile. "They just haven't been offered it yet, Wayne. There aren't any exceptions to the rule. Anyway, you can't have it both ways. You said the leak could be in the police department, and they're the two the D.A.'s been keeping informed."

"Cops don't work in a vacuum, Andrew. Their supervisor knows whatever they know, other cops overhear conversations and have access to records. It could be anyone in their division."

After thinking this over, Mello conceded the point with a nod. "So what's my status? If there was a warrant out on me, I assume those guys in front would have served it."

"There's no warrant—yet. My deal with Coleman is that if you agree to testify, we check you into the Red Hart Motel when we get to L.A. You'll stay there, under guard, until it's time to appear before the grand jury. If you don't agree to testify, we drive straight to Parker Center, where you'll be booked on conspiracy to commit murder. How shall I instruct the driver?"

Mello smiled bleakly. "Tell him to drive to the motel."

Giving his client an approving nod, the lawyer leaned forward to slide open the glass partition. "Officer Phelps," he said. "When we hit Los Angeles, our destination is the Red Hart Motel."

Chapter III

WHEN A RINGING noise awakened her, the redhead groped for the alarm clock without opening her eyes and pushed in the button. When the ringing continued, she opened one eye, focused it on the nightstand next to her, then lifted the bedside phone.

"Umph?" she said.

"Cindy?" a male voice asked in her ear.

The redhead's other eye popped open. "No, I am not Cindy," she said crossly.

"Oh, sorry. Maybe I have the wrong number. I was trying to reach Dave Starsky's apartment."

"You've got it, but I'm still not Cindy. Just who is Cindy, if you don't mind?"

There was a long pause before the male voice said, "The cleaning lady. Now that I think of it, she wouldn't be there this morning, because she only comes in on Mondays. May I speak to Starsky, please?"

The redhead jabbed her elbow into the ribs of the man next to her. Dave Starsky, who was already awake and had been listening, emitted a pained grunt and sat up. Bare to the waist, wearing only pajama bottoms, he was a leanly muscled man in his late twenties with curling, dark-brown hair and blue eyes.

Handing him the phone, the redhead said, "Some dude wants to talk to you about your cleaning lady."

"Yeah?" Starsky said into the phone.

The voice of his partner, Detective Ken Hutchinson, said, "Sorry to wake you so early, Starsk, but you'll need an early start because you have to pick me up at home this morning. I'm not going to the gym."

Starsky looked across the redhead at the alarm clock on the nightstand on her side of the bed. Although it was only 6:30, mid-June sun was already struggling through the blinds.

"How come you're not going to the gym?" he asked.

"I have some company."

After a period of silence, Starsky said, "So have I. How come I have to cut my visit with my company short and drive clear to Venice just so you can visit longer with your company?"

"Don't be unreasonable, Starsk," Hutchinson said. "I just did *you* a favor. I explained to your guest that Cindy was your cleaning lady."

"Thanks a bunch, buddy. If you hadn't phoned, the explanation would have been unnecessary."

"Picky, picky," Hutch said, and hung up.

Starsky handed the phone back to the redhead, who sat up to receive it and replace it in its cradle. She had a pretty, heart-shaped face with large green eyes, and a firm, lovely figure. She had been sleeping nude. She leaned over to give Starsky a kiss on the cheek.

"Who was that?" she asked.

"My partner, Hutch. I have to leave early because I have to pick him up at home instead of at Vinnie's gym in our district. Usually he works out every morning."

He swung out of bed and headed for the bathroom, shedding his pajama bottoms and kicking them aside en route.

"Why did he think your cleaning lady would be here so early in the morning?" she asked.

Pausing in the bathroom doorway, he said, "She always comes early. And this is Tuesday, her regular day. Naturally Hutch assumed it was her. Probably she's late because her arthritis has been acting up again."

"Your friend Hutch said she came on Mondays," the girl said suspiciously.

"He never can keep dates straight. He's a little retarded."

He went on into the bathroom and closed the door. Bouncing from bed, she reopened it and joined Starsky who was standing outside the shower stall with one hand held in the spray, testing the temperature.

"How old is Cindy?" she demanded.

"I'm in a terrible hurry, Gwen," Starsky said. "I'll tell you all about her later."

He stepped into the shower stall and closed the door. Immediately it reopened, Gwen stepped in, and pulled the door closed again.

"Hey, it's crowded in here," he complained.

"Crowded is nice," she told him. Lifting the soap from its recess, she handed it to him. "We can save time by washing each other's backs." She turned hers.

"I have a feeling it will end in lost time," he said resignedly. "I also have a feeling we're going to miss breakfast."

Nevertheless he began soaping her back.

It was another half-hour before they got around to

dressing, which was about the time the alarm would have gone off if Hutch hadn't phoned. It didn't take Gwen long to dress because all she put on was white shorts, a green halter, thong sandals, and a thin white sweater. Starsky donned faded Levi's, Hush Puppies, a T-shirt, a worn blue Windbreaker, and a knitted Los Angeles Rams warm-up cap. Taking a .38 automatic from the drawer of a nightstand, he pulled up the back of his Windbreaker and thrust the gun under his belt in the middle of his back.

On the way down to the basement garage, Gwen said, "I'm hungry."

"The buddy-buddy shower was your idea," he said. "We would have had plenty of time for breakfast."

"I wasn't hungry then. Probably the exercise gave me an appetite."

Starsky's car was a bright-red Torino with a foot-wide white stripe running across the top from side to side just in front of the rear window, down the sides, and then forward to taper to points at the hood. As he unlocked it, he said to Gwen, who was waiting on the opposite side of the car for him to open her door, "I haven't time to run you home. I'll drop you at the bus stop a block from here."

Staring at him across the top of the car, she said with mild outrage, "Not take me home! After all we've been to each other!"

Getting in, Starsky reached across to unlock the other door. As the redhead slid in next to him, he said, "You're the one who made me late."

"That's the second time you've blamed me," she said indignantly. "I suppose you just gave in out of a sense of duty."

"I try to be a considerate host," he told her. "Even when my guests are pushy."

She pinched him in a vulnerable spot.

When he pulled the Torino up in front of the bus stop, she sat looking at him for a moment. "How old is Cindy?" she finally asked.

"I never inquired, but her age looks about sixty-two in a mirror."

"Oh," she said with a relieved little laugh. Climbing from the car, but leaving the door open, she peered back in. "You'll phone me?"

"Of course."

Suddenly she frowned. "What do you mean, her age looks about sixty-two in a mirror?"

"You see it backward there," he said.

He reached across to pull the door closed. As he drove off, she yelled after him, "You mean she's twenty-six, you louse!"

Starsky put his left hand over his right shoulder and wiggled his fingers in a wave of good-bye.

It was 7:30 when Starsky pulled the Torino in next to Hutch's little canalside cottage in Venice. The small one-story building, surrounded by a white picket fence that almost bordered the edge of the canal on one side, belonged on a picture postcard. Starsky sometimes thought of getting something similar for himself, but he was too much of a city boy ever to be happy in such a quiet environment for more than short vacation periods. His mid-city apartment suited his nature much better.

Starsky punched the doorbell, then went in without waiting for an invitation. The main room was a combination living room and sleeping area, with a double bed dominating the far end, and a sofa, chairs, and end tables spread about. Starsky was used to seeing the bed unmade, books and magazines scattered on the end tables, and clothing draped over chairs. Just inside he paused to gaze with astonishment at a neatly made bed and a spotless room.

In the kitchen off the main room to the right he found Hutch and a bright-eyed, black-haired girl in the uniform of an airline stewardess seated together at the breakfast bar. The girl had a plate before her with the remnants of bacon and eggs on it, and was sipping a cup of coffee. Hutch had nothing in front of him but a glass half full of something that looked like slightly gray milk.

Like Starsky, Kenneth Hutchinson was in his late twenties, had blue eyes, and was leanly muscled. But there the resemblance stopped. About two inches taller than Starsky's five feet eleven, he had blond hair and a sort of genteel handsomeness. In well-pressed slacks and an expensive sport shirt, he looked more like a Beverly Hills socialite than a cop. Just as Starsky was obviously a product of the streets, Hutch Hutchinson obviously had "breeding."

"Morning, Starsk," Hutch said. "This is Gwendolyn Cole. Dave Starsky, Gwen."

"Hi, Dave," the brunette said, smiling at him.

Pulling off his Rams cap, Starsky said, "Hi. That's a coincidence. The girl who answered the phone at my place had the identical name."

"Gwendolyn Cole?" Hutch asked with raised brows.

"Just Gwendolyn." He looked at the half-empty glass before Hutch. "Is that some of that awful health breakfast you mix up, with goat's milk and dessicated liver in it?"

"It's not awful, it's delicious. And very healthful."

Starsky made a face. "I was hoping to bum some breakfast, but I'm not drinking that glop."

"I woke you up in plenty of time to have breakfast," Hutch said.

"I got sidetracked."

"I'll fix you some breakfast," the girl volunteered.

"We don't have the ingredients for what he eats," Hutch said. "For breakfast he likes things like cold pizza and root beer."

"Only when it's available," Starsky told the girl. "I also eat bacon and eggs."

"Not this morning, you don't," Hutch informed him. "We've got just about time to make our district before eight. You can catch a snack on the fly somewhere after we log in."

Draining his glass, Hutch got up and walked into the other room, where he could be seen putting on a

shoulder harness with attached gun holster, then slipping a plaid sports jacket over it.

"Sorry, Dave," the girl said. "I would have been glad
to cook for you."

"It's all right," Starsky assured her. "I feel more
like a chile dog than bacon and eggs anyway, and
there's a place on our beat that makes them."

"For breakfast?" she said with a slightly seasick
expression on her face.

Coming back into the kitchen, Hutch said, "His
stomach's going to fall out by the time he's forty."
He leaned down to give the girl a quick kiss. "Lock
the door when you leave, hon."

"Sure," she said. "That'll be a while, because I'm
going to do the breakfast dishes."

Outside, as they climbed into the Torino, Starsky
asked, "How do you get girls to do the housework?
My Gwendolyn left my place in a mess."

"Charm," Hutch said. "You have to have charm."

Chapter IV

AS STARSKY GUNNED the Torino, Hutch said, "Aren't
you going to read me off the checklist?"

"You know it by heart," Starsky said. Pulling a
small clipboard from atop the sun visor, he dropped it
on the seat between them. "Here, check it over after
you check out the equipment."

Hutch opened the glove compartment, peered into it,
and said, "Shells, flares, tear-gas grenades." From beneath his seat, he pulled out a rack that slid in and
out on rollers, like a drawer. It contained a variety of
items. Hutch picked up a riot gun and slid back the

bolt far enough to make sure a shell was in the chamber. Replacing it, he examined two citizen's band portable radios, switched a flashlight on and off, then picked up a police-car flasher that could be attached to the roof by suction cups. He briefly switched it on then off again, and put it back in the rack. Shoving the rack back under the seat, he picked up the clipboard, scanned the equipment list, and replaced it atop the visor.

"Everything okay?" Starsky asked.

"Like Swiss watches." Hutch reached up under the dashboard and brought out a thick notebook anchored to a chain. "Anything new in this?"

"Not since yesterday."

Hutch riffled through the wanted posters, record sheets, and police bulletins anyway. He stopped when he came to a record sheet containing the front and profile mug shots of a heavy-featured man with a totally bald head.

"Curly Dobbs," he said. "He's one creature we better watch when they let Andy Mello out next week."

"We'll have to watch a hundred creatures."

"Maybe, but Kester's chief hatchet man is Curly. I'll bet he's the one who arranged Whitey Bomosuto's disappearing act."

"Not with me, you won't," Starsky said. "That's my bet, too."

Hutch closed the book and shoved it back under the dashboard.

When they reached their cruising district in downtown Los Angeles, Hutch reached beneath the dashboard again and drew out a radio microphone. Pressing the transmit button, he said, "Zebra Three to Control One. Come in, Control One."

From the radio speaker came, "Control One to Zebra Three. Go ahead."

"Log us on the street and rolling," Hutch said. He glanced at his bare wrist, looked surprised, released the transmit button, and said to Starsky, "I forgot to put on my watch. What time is it?"

"Mine's on my dresser," Starsky said. "It quit running."

Hutch glanced at the dash clock, which registered ten after six.

In an apologetic voice Starsky said, "It loses five minutes a day, and I haven't set it for a few weeks."

The radio dispatcher, tired of waiting for Hutch to give his log-in time, said, "You're logged in at eight hundred hours and three minutes, Zebra Three."

"Check," Hutch said. "Over and out."

Replacing the microphone, Hutch set the dash clock for three minutes after eight.

Most of the time, cruising in an undercover police car is dull work. The Torino cruised down one street and up another in their assigned district. Hutch's gaze took in every person and each event taking place on the right side of the street, while Starsky surveyed the left. But nothing worthy of police action happened during the first hour.

As it neared nine, Starsky said, "How about a coffee break? I still haven't had any breakfast."

"Okay with me," Hutch said. "Let's combine it with business. Swing by Huggy Bear's and we'll see if he has any new dope on Kester's plans for Mello."

"I kind of felt like a chile dog," Starsky said.

"Give your stomach a break and go to Huggy's," Hutch advised. "It'll last longer."

"Well, okay," Starsky agreed. "One of Angie's omelettes would hit the spot, too." He made a left turn at the next corner.

The Internal Revenue Service, the State Alcoholic Beverages Control Board, and the Department of Motor Vehicles all knew Huggy Bear's real name, but no one else did, including his bank and his employees. He signed his paychecks "Huggy Bear." He was the owner and manager of the restaurant-bar in downtown Los Angeles that bore his name. He was also a valuable source of information for Starsky and Hutch, because his contacts ran deep into the underworld. He was not an informer. It was tacitly understood that

nothing incriminating to his underworld friends
would ever be forthcoming from him, but for general
information about what was going on in the underworld he was a fountain of information.

Huggy Bear was tending bar when Starsky and
Hutch arrived. At nine in the morning this didn't require much effort, because the breakfast trade was
minimal. They found him seated on a stool next to
the cash register, morosely regarding his single customer, an elderly white man drinking beer at the far
end of the bar.

Huggy Bear was a tall, lean black man with close-
cropped hair and an elfin expression. Today he was
dressed rather conservatively, for him. He wore solid
bright-pink slacks and a matching shirt; usually he
went in for loud stripes and checks.

Waving a languorous hand at the two detectives,
Huggy Bear said, "Morning, good buddies. I hope
you are here for cash business instead of just to pick
my brain, 'cause things are kind of slow."

The detectives seated themselves opposite him, in
the center of the bar. Starsky said, "We're here for
some of both. I haven't had any breakfast."

"Angie ain't here yet," Huggy Bear said. "Should be
along any minute. Want a beer while you're waiting?"

Starsky looked pained. "Your dietary ideas are
worse than Hutch's. Beer before breakfast?"

Getting up, he went over to a candy machine near
the door, dropped coins into it, and pulled a lever. He
looked pleasantly surprised when a candy bar dropped
into the tray at the bottom.

Peeling it as he returned to the bar, he said, "I'm
starting to get the hang of machines. Usually nothing
happens until I pull at least three levers. Today I got
my first choice."

"You're going to eat that *before* breakfast?" Hutch
inquired, examining the candy bar with distaste.

"Do I complain about all that organic health food
glop you eat?" Starsky demanded.

"Constantly."

The side door from the alley opened; a small black man entered and walked briskly across the room into the kitchen.

"There's Angie," Huggy Bear said. "What you want?"

"Fudge omelette and coffee."

"A *fudge* omelette," Hutch said. "What the devil is a fudge omelette?"

"One with fudge in it," Starsky said. "Angie makes a delicious one. I gave him the recipe."

"You want anything?" Huggy Bear asked Hutch.

"Just coffee," Hutch said, looking slightly ill.

Huggy Bear descended from his stool and went into the kitchen. Starsky began to eat his candy bar. Hutch watched him disapprovingly.

Huggy Bear returned carrying a tray with two cups of coffee, cream, and sugar on it. He unloaded the tray onto the counter and climbed back onto his stool.

"How about another beer?" the elderly man at the end of the counter asked.

Sighing, Huggy Bear descended again to give him a beer, rang up the sale, and resumed his seat. By then Starsky had finished his candy bar and was taking a cautious sip of his coffee. Hutch let his sit there cooling.

"Any further scuttlebutt about Kester's contract on Mello?" Hutch asked Huggy Bear.

"Not a peep," the black man said. "It's tightened up. Which may mean Kester heard there were rumors and clamped the lid."

"Got any guesses about who got the contract?" Starsky asked.

Huggy Bear pursed his lips. "Curly Dobbs seems logical. He usually gets the big ones. But that's just an off-the-cuff guess."

Glancing at the clock on the wall behind the bar, Hutch asked, "That thing right?"

Huggy Bear looked up at the clock, which showed 9:06, then at the wristwatch he was wearing. "Minute and a half fast."

"How do you know your watch is right?" Starsky asked.

"This watch is *never* wrong. This here is a precision timepiece like you never saw before." Stretching the expansion band in order to slip it off, he leaned forward to hand it to Starsky.

It was an expensive Swiss-movement watch, with a date indicator.

"Look at the back," Huggy Bear said.

There was a crystal on the back as well as on the front. Beneath it were hundreds of tiny glowing dots on a black field, and in one corner there was a tiny crescent about an eighth of an inch long.

"That's the night sky over Southern California and the phase of the moon," Huggy Bear explained. "If you look close, you can make out all the constellations. You can set it to get the sky in any section of the world."

Starsky said, "Holy cow! You can make out the Big and Little Dippers!"

"Let's see it," Hutch said, holding out his hand.

Reluctantly Starsky relinquished the watch. As Hutch examined it, Starsky asked Huggy Bear, "How much a watch like that worth?"

"My buddy said it cost fifteen hundred new. I took it for a debt he owed me."

"How much a debt?"

"Three hundred sixty dollars. Couple of years back his ex-wife was gonna have him cast in the slammer for being behind in child support. I bailed him out and he never got ahead enough to pay me back. Other day I run into him and leaned on him a little, and he offered me the watch to square it. I needed it like a hole in the head. Got a dozen watches already I took to square loans. But I figured it was the only way I'd ever collect."

"You want to sell it?" Starsky asked.

"Sure, if you got three hundred sixty clams."

Taking a money clip from his pocket, Starsky

counted the bills. "I got two seventy." He looked at Hutch. "You got ninety on you?"

Hutch took a wallet from his breast pocket and checked the contents. "Exactly. But then how can you pay for breakfast?"

"I'll charge it."

Huggy Bear pointed to a sign over the cash register reading: ABSOLUTELY NO CREDIT.

"Okay," Starsky said. "Then I'll charge the watch." He took it back from Hutch and slipped it on his wrist.

"I can make one exception," Huggy Bear said hurriedly.

A bell from the kitchen sounded.

"Your omelette's ready," Huggy Bear said, getting down from his stool. "You can be counting out the three hundred sixty while I get it."

Chapter V

ABOUT 11 A.M. the dispatcher called Zebra Three and instructed Starsky and Hutch to come in to Parker Center and report to Captain Dobey. They walked into his office at 11:15. The captain was seated behind his desk, dictating a letter to a civilian secretary seated alongside the desk. He waved to the two detectives to be seated until he finished. They took side-by-side chairs against the wall.

Captain Harold Dobey was a large black man in his late forties, an inch short of six feet and weighing 225 pounds. He had a round, intelligent face that seldom smiled, and wore a black mustache. A conservative dresser, today he was wearing a blue serge suit with a white shirt and a dark-blue necktie.

Starsky and Hutch barely glanced at the captain, because their attention was focused on the secretary. She was a slim, attractive blonde in her late twenties dressed in a powder-blue miniskirt and matching sleeveless sweater. There were interesting bumps in the sweater.

Finishing his dictation, Dobey said, "No rush on that, Terry, but I want it out today. Before you start it, will you bring us some coffee?" He looked at Starsky and Hutch. "You want coffee?"

Both indicated they did, and specified black.

"You two know Terry Evers?" the captain asked.

Hutch said, "We've talked on the phone a couple of times."

Starsky said, "Seen her around. How are you, Terry?"

"Fine, Officer Hutchinson," she said. She looked at Hutch. "Morning, Officer Starsky."

Hutch said in a pained voice, "I'm Hutch." He jerked a thumb at his partner. "He's Starsky."

"Oh," the girl said. "Sorry."

As she got up from her chair and carried her notebook from the room, Starsky looked up at the wall clock and made an elaborate show of checking it against his watch. He said, "Your clock is about twenty seconds slow, Captain."

Dobey stared at him. "You got that watch connected by radio waves to the Naval Observatory?"

"This here is a three-hundred-and-sixty-dollar watch," Starsky told him. "Actually a fifteen-hundred-dollar one, but I only paid three sixty for it. It's accurate to the split second. Plus, look at this."

Slipping off the watch, he carried it over to the desk and held it so the captain could see the back. "That's a picture of the night sky over Los Angeles, and the phase of the moon."

After gazing at it for a few moments, Dobey said, "Couldn't you just look up?"

Starsky looked at him blankly, then said, "Not if you were indoors."

Hutch said, "You could look out the window."

"The pair of you are a couple of killjoys," Starsky groused. He slipped the watch back on and returned to his seat.

"What was it you wanted to see us about, Captain?" Hutch asked.

"Andy Mello's out."

Both detectives looked surprised. Hutch said, "I thought he wasn't due for parole until next week."

"That was deliberately false information released for security reasons at the request of Don Coleman. At the moment Mello's in a motel under guard, but Coleman wants us to find somewhere safer. That's the job for you two. Find a spot where it will be easy to protect him, and we'll transfer him this afternoon."

Terry Evers re-entered, carrying two Styrofoam cups in her left hand and one in her right. She began passing them around.

"Where do they have Mello now?" Starsky asked. "Oh, thank you, Terry."

The girl gave him a smile, handed a cup to Hutch, and returned his thanks with another smile.

"At the Red Hart Motel on Olympic," Captain Dobey said. "Darrow and Phelps are guarding him, but I want you there too for the transfer. You two can lead the way to the safe house while they follow in another car with Mello. Thanks, Terry."

"You're welcome, Captain."

Hutch asked, "Has he agreed to testify?"

"He's not only agreed, he's going to give Kester to Coleman on a Murder One."

"Anything else, Captain?" the blond secretary asked.

"No, not now."

"You did remember that my dental appointment is this afternoon, didn't you, Captain?"

"Dental appointment?" he said, looking up at her with a frown.

"I told you last week, and you said it was okay. It's at two P.M. I probably won't be out before three-thirty, which means it would be after four before I got back here. So is it all right if I just don't come back at all after lunch?"

"All right," the captain assented. "You'd better get those letters typed up before noon, then."

"Yes, sir," she said, and left the room for the second time.

Back in the outer office, she made a brief phone call before beginning to type.

At noon Terry Evers took the elevator to the basement garage, walked up the ramp to the parking lot reserved for Parker Center personnel, and climbed into a two-year-old Volkswagen. She drove straight to an office building on Figueroa Street. Taking an elevator to the fifth floor, she entered a door lettered KESTER ENTERPRISES.

A middle-aged female receptionist sat behind a desk in a small but lushly furnished reception room. A huge bald-headed man in a business suit sat on a sofa reading a racing form. He glanced up at Terry briefly, then went back to his form.

Terry said to the receptionist, "Mr. Kester is expecting me. I'm Terry."

"Oh, yes, Miss—ah—Terry," the woman said. "The door at the far end of the hall."

The blonde went past the desk to the hall. She passed a number of open office doors, through which she could see shirt-sleeved men working at desks or talking on phones. At the end of the hall was a door lettered in gold leaf: OFFICE OF THE PRESIDENT—HARRY J. KESTER.

Terry knocked, entered, closed the door behind her. The office was nearly as large as the reception room. There was an oval glass-topped desk containing three phones and an interoffice communicator, a bar in one corner, a leather-covered sofa and three leather-covered easy chairs.

Harry Kester, seated behind the desk, gave her a

welcoming smile, but it didn't reach his eyes. "This better be as important as you said," he greeted her. "Coming here could blow your cover sky high."

"Captain Dobey thinks I'm at the dentist, and nobody here but you knows who I am," Terry said. "This was too hot to tell you over the phone." She seated herself in the easy chair nearest the desk. "Andrew Mello is out of prison, is under police protection, and has agreed to testify against you."

The racket boss's eyes narrowed. "For what?"

"Murder One."

Kester looked startled. "Who?"

She shook her head. "I didn't get that."

After a moment's reflection Kester said, "There's nothing he could pin on me without incriminating himself."

"Maybe the D.A.'s offered him general immunity, not just for Morgan."

"Yeah," Kester said thoughtfully. "He must have. You know where they have the old man?"

"At the Red Hart Motel on Olympic Boulevard at the moment. With two cops guarding him. They're planning to move him to some safer place this afternoon."

"When this afternoon?"

She shrugged. "No time was set. Dobey assigned a couple of cops to find a safe house, but they only started looking about an hour ago."

"What cops?"

"Starsky and Hutchinson."

Kester made a face. "Jesus, that complicates things. We'll have to get to Mello before they move him, because that pair never does things halfway. They'll find a fortress."

"They're going to be in on the moving of him, too. They'll lead the way to the safe house, while the other two cops follow with Mello in another car. That will be Darrow and Phelps."

Kester considered for a moment, then pressed the

switch of the intercom box and said, "Ellie, do you have a map of Los Angeles?"

The receptionist's voice said, "Yes, sir."

"Send Curly in with it."

"Yes, sir," she repeated.

Switching off the machine, Kester took the yellow-pages directory from a bottom desk drawer and thumbed through the motel listings. There were six pages of them. He found the listing for the Red Hart Motel, jotted down the address, and put the book back in the drawer.

The door opened and the bald man who had been reading a racing form came in. Crossing to the desk, he handed Kester a folded map. Kester spread it open on his desk.

"Come around here, Curly," he said.

The huge bald man rounded the desk to peer over the seated man's shoulder. After studying the map for a few moments, Kester pointed to a spot with his index finger.

"This is the fifteen-hundred block of Olympic Boulevard," he said. "There's a place called the Red Hart Motel there. I want you to go find out if there is a pay phone nearby from which cars leaving the motel can be seen."

"Okay," the big man said agreeably.

With his index finger still on the spot, Kester said, "You'll notice Ninth Street is the first parallel street north of Olympic just there, and Tenth is the first one south. Find another pay phone in that same block on one or the other of those, and mark down the phone number."

"What's that for?"

"Andy Mello is under police guard at the Red Hart Motel. Sometime this afternoon they're going to move him." He looked up at Terry. "I suppose you have to get back to work after your pretended dental appointment."

She shook her head. "I have the afternoon off."

"Good," he said in a pleased voice. "That simplifies things. Curly, she'll be watching the motel. You'll be waiting by the second phone. When Mello takes off, she'll phone you to tell you which direction he goes."

The bald man looked at Terry. They had never seen each other before, but obviously Kester had no intention of introducing them. Curly didn't ask who she was.

Returning his attention to Kester, Curly asked, "How many cops will be guarding him?"

"Four. Two in a lead vehicle, the other two in the car with Mello behind that."

The big man frowned. "How am I supposed to handle four cops?"

"Hit-and-run," Kester said. "You're going to be riding on the back of Dippy Marrs' motorcycle. You should be able to zoom in there, blast Mello, and get the hell out again before they even know what's happening."

After considering this, Curly let a slow grin form on his face. "Should be like shooting fish in a barrel," he said.

"Just in case it isn't, we'll have a backup car tail you by a half-block, ready to move in if necessary."

"Sounds even better," Curly said.

"Okay, get humping," Kester told him. "I don't know how much time we have before they move Mello. Get back here with the dope as fast as you can."

"Check," the bald man said.

He threw another glance at Terry on the way out, but didn't say anything to her.

Kester switched on the intercom again. "Ellie, get Dippy Marrs over here fast. Whatever he's doing, including eating lunch, tell him to drop it and run. And to come on his motorbike."

"Yes, sir," she said.

Switching the machine off again, he said to Terry, "You haven't had lunch, have you?"

She shook her head.

"It'll be a while before Curly gets back. I'll have

something brought in." Opening a desk drawer, he took
out a stack of restaurant menus and pushed them
across the desk to her. "Take your pick."

"All these choices?" she asked.

"They're all nearby, and all deliver. Like Mexican
food?"

"Very much."

"Café Valdez has good food."

She found the appropriate menu and selected a
taco with rice. Kester ordered a burrito. Curly got back
before the lunches were delivered.

"There's a public phone booth right across the street
from the Red Hart Motel," he announced. "And another in the middle of the block on Ninth. Here's the
number of it."

He handed a slip of paper to Kester, who glanced
at it, then shoved it across the desk to Terry.

"You understand what you're supposed to do?" he
asked.

"Yes, I understand."

Curly asked, "You get in touch with Dippy?"

"I sent for him. While we're waiting, stick your head
in Deeks' office and tell him I want him and Thorn
to back you up. You can explain the setup to him and
tell him where to be with the backup car."

"Roger," the bald man said, and left the room
again.

The intercom buzzed and Kester flicked it on. The
receptionist's voice said, "A delivery boy is here with
two lunches, Mr. Kester. Shall I send him in?"

Throwing the speaker switch, Kester said, "No. Pay
him out of petty cash, give him a two-dollar tip and
bring them in yourself."

Switching the speaker off again, he said to Terry,
"The less people see you in here, the better."

Chapter VI

TERRY EVERS PARKED her Volkswagen a quarter block away from the motel, on the opposite side of the street. She had a long wait. It was 3:30 P.M. before the red-and-white Torino appeared and turned in at the driveway that circled the motel building. As soon as it had turned in, she climbed from the car, walked to the phone booth directly across from the motel, dropped a coin and dialed.

There was an instant answer. "Yeah?"

"Starsky and Hutch just arrived," she said. "Hang on."

"All right."

She stood with the phone held to her ear, watching the exit end of the driveway.

Starsky slowly piloted the Torino along the drive, peering at the numbers on doors as he passed them. He finally nosed in next to a black limousine parked in front of unit 23. Cutting the engine, he looked at his new watch.

"We told the D.A. three-thirty sharp," he said with satisfaction. "To the second, baby. Precision."

Hutch said, "Starsky, I hate that watch."

Starsky looked at him in astonishment. "How can you hate a three-hundred-and-sixty-dollar watch?"

"Because you keep telling me how much it cost."

Starsky examined him quizzically. "Sure it isn't the job you hate?"

After considering, Hutch nodded. "Maybe. You telling me you like squiring a hood around?"

"Oh, I don't know. Andrew Mello's no ordinary hood. Look at his credits. Pushing dope to eleven-year-old kids, cornering the market on everything from union-busting to prostitution."

"I guess we should feel honored," Hutch agreed. "It isn't every day we can rush such a public-spirited citizen to safety so that he'll live long enough to testify before the grand jury."

Starsky nodded. "Especially since the only way they could bust him was on income-tax evasion."

Two men who obviously had been watching from the windows of unit 23 stepped outside. Starsky and Hutch knew both of them well. The tall, lanky man was Sergeant Ken Darrow. The heavy-shouldered, thick-waisted one was Detective Barry Phelps. The men waved their hands toward Starsky and Hutch, then looked all around. Satisfied that all was clear, Sergeant Darrow reopened the motel door. Two other men stepped outdoors. One was Andrew Mello, immaculately dressed in a gray pinstripe suit and a pearl-gray homburg. The other was District Attorney Donald Coleman, a lean, aggressive-looking man in his mid-thirties with close-cropped hair and an executive air about him.

Starsky and Hutch got out of the Torino and moved toward the group. As soon as he spotted them, Andrew Mello stepped behind the thick-bodied Barry Phelps.

"It's all right," Coleman said to him. "They're with us. Detectives Dave Starsky and Ken Hutchinson."

Moving out from behind Phelps, the ex-racket boss examined the pair dourly. "I've heard of them. How come you wanted them?"

"Because they're the best," Coleman said. Turning to Starsky and Hutch, he asked, "You find a safe house?"

Hutch said, "Yes, sir, Mr. Coleman."

Andrew Mello said to Coleman, "You figure you need your best men just to move me to a safe house?"

"Let's not take any chances, Mello."

Detective Phelps held open the rear door of the

limousine for Mello to get in back, then climbed in after him. Sergeant Darrow got in front to drive.

Donald Coleman said to Starsky and Hutch, "I'll ride with you. Is this place far?"

"Over near the courthouse," Starsky said. "We figured the less distance he had to go to testify, the easier security would be."

"Good thinking," the district attorney said.

He climbed in the back of the Torino, Hutch got in front, and Starsky slipped behind the wheel. As he drove toward the street exit, the black limousine followed closely behind.

Across the street Terry Evers said into the phone, "They just came out and turned east, in the direction of the Harbor Freeway."

Moving east on Olympic Boulevard, the Torino and the trailing limousine crossed Valencia, then Albany. As the lead car neared Blaine Street, just before the freeway, a motorcycle shot across Olympic from the left side of the intersection, cutting in front of the Torino. Two men wearing black leather jackets, motorcycle helmets, and goggles were on the cycle. The three men in the car got the fleeting impression that the driver was skinny and his passenger rather oversized, but it happened so fast that none of them saw either man clearly.

As Starsky hit the brakes so hard that the car skidded, the big man on the rear of the motorcycle fired two shots through the windshield. Both miraculously passed between Starsky and Hutch without hitting them, and exited by the rear window without hitting the man in the back seat either. The motorcycle made an S around the right side of the Torino, across the front of the limousine, and then along its left side. The gunman blasted two shots through the windshield of the limousine, then a third through the back-seat side window.

Starsky and Hutch tumbled out opposite sides of the Torino with drawn guns. As Hutch ran toward the limousine, Starsky dropped to one knee, holding his gun with both hands, and fired twice at the speeding motorcycle.

Although Starsky was a pretty good shot, there was more luck than skill in both shots meeting target, because by then the motorcycle was a good half-block beyond. Starsky knew he hit the man on the back of the machine with the first shot, because he could see him wince. He knew he hit the rear tire with the second one, because it blew. The cycle skidded onto its side, throwing the passenger clear. The driver stayed with it as it slid along the pavement a good two-hundred feet, ending up with his left leg pinned beneath the machine when it finally came to rest in the right-hand gutter.

Hutch peered into the limousine. Like the Torino, it had two bullet holes in the windshield and both slugs had exited through the rear window. In addition the left back-seat side window was shattered. Neither detective had been hit, but Andrew Mello was clutching his right shoulder and blood was seeping through his fingers.

"Is it bad?" Hutch asked Phelps.

"He'll live," the heavy-shouldered detective said.

Swinging toward the driver, Hutch said, "Get him to Memorial."

Nodding, Darrow shifted into *drive* and swung around the Torino to head for the Harbor Freeway. Hutch ran back to jump into the front seat of the Torino just as Starsky slid behind the wheel. Don Coleman, pointing back through the rear window, said in a high-pitched voice, "Get those two!"

"Forget it," Starsky said. "We stay with Mello."

The Torino roared after the limousine.

Grabbing the microphone, Hutch said into it, "Zebra Three to Control One. Come in, Control One."

The radio said, "Control One here. Go ahead, Zebra Three."

"Mello's limousine was ambushed and Mello is wounded. Limo en route Southern Memorial Hospital. Assailants, both injured, lying in street on Olympic between Blaine and Albany. Both white males, dressed in black leather jackets, motorcycle helmets, and goggles. Have them picked up, but tell the backups to approach with care. Also, we want the damaged motorcycle they were riding on impounded."

As they followed the limousine up the on-ramp of the freeway, the dispatcher said, "Roger, Zebra Three. Will do."

Hutch hung up the microphone.

"Is he hurt bad?" Coleman asked from the back seat. "Is he going to live?"

"Phelps said he will," Hutch told him.

Back on Olympic Boulevard, several cars had stopped to offer assistance to the injured men. But before anyone could get out of them, a blue Ford sedan turned right from Blaine, shot around the halted traffic and screeched to a stop beside the oversized passenger of the motorcycle. He was just climbing painfully to his feet with blood seeping from a hole in his left shoulder. A man jumped out of the front passenger seat of the Ford, jerked open the rear door, and shoved the wounded man inside. Slamming the door, he jumped back in front as his driver zoomed away. Two hundred feet later, the Ford again screeched to a halt alongside the wrecked motorcycle. Again the man jumped from the front seat and jerked open the rear door. Running over to the motorcycle, he heaved it off of the pinned-down leg of the driver, helped the injured man to his feet, and supported him as he hobbled over to the car. When he was in the back seat with the other wounded man and the door was closed, he jumped back in front and the Ford took off with a squeal.

In addition to the stopped cars, a half-dozen pedestrians on the street had been heading toward the scene of the accident when the blue Ford came along. Unlike the occupants of the halted cars, they had witnessed the gunplay preceding the spill and knew it wasn't simply an accident. One of the pedestrians, an elderly man, jotted down the license number of the Ford.

At the hospital all four police officers stayed on guard outside the emergency room while the district attorney went upstairs to the desk to arrange for a private room that would meet security requirements. When he came back, he announced that he had gotten a fifth-floor corner room on a deadend corridor. He asked Starsky and Hutch if they wanted to check it out to make sure it was safe before Mello was moved to it.

Hutch said, "We'll stick with Mello and check it out after we get him up there. If it isn't safe, we'll move him to a room that is."

It was some time before the two doctors who were working on the wounded man came from the emergency room. One moved on, but the other paused to say to the district attorney, "Clean wound. He'll be all right."

"Can he talk?" Coleman asked.

"Oh, yes. He's lightly sedated, but not enough to make him irrational."

A nurse wheeled the patient out of the emergency room on a gurney. Mello was covered by a sheet, but his arms were free. His right shoulder was heavily bandaged and the tube running from a bottle of blood was taped to his left wrist.

At that moment Captain Dobey came hurrying along the basement corridor. Looking at the wounded man, he asked, "How is he?"

"As well as can be expected, Captain," Mello growled in a slightly thickened voice.

A slight smile formed on the captain's usually serious face. "I guess you'll live, Andrew."

"It takes better shooting than that motorcycle punk's to cash me in, Harold. Three shots, and he only pinked me once."

The nurse wheeled the gurney toward the elevator. The four detectives fell in as escorts, two on either side. Coleman and Dobey trailed behind.

"What happened?" Dobey asked the district attorney. "All I got was a report that he'd been ambushed."

Coleman gave him a brief rundown of events, finishing just as they reached the elevator. There was a short wait there because the car was on an upper floor.

Coleman said to Dobey, "Your man Starsky shoots a lot better than the would-be assassin."

Seeing by his expression that Starsky had heard the remark, Dobey said, "All my men shoot pretty good. Starsky's about average."

Chapter VII

AS A MATTER of routine all four detectives stood facing the elevator, shielding Mello with their bodies on the remote chance that another gunman would be on the elevator when the door opened. There wasn't anyone on it when it did.

Holding the door open with one hand, Hutch said to the nurse, "We're going to do this the safe way, just in case the gentleman who wants Mr. Mello dead guessed where we were bringing him and sent some other people to look in on him. My partner and I will ride up to fifth while you wait here with the patient. I'll leave him to cover the fifth-floor hallway, while I bring the car back down and make sure nobody enters the elevator en route."

"Whatever you say, Officer," she said, smiling at him.

These precautions proved unnecessary. Ten minutes later the wounded man was wheeled into his private fifth-floor room without incident. Captain Dobey instructed Darrow and Phelps to stand guard duty in the corridor, but everyone else went in with the patient. Starsky and Hutch immediately went over to check the two windows, leaning out to make sure there was no possible way to gain access to the room by that route. Don Coleman picked up the phone and gave a number to the switchboard operator.

The nurse rolled the gurney over next to the bed, stripped the sheet from the patient to disclose that he was in hospital pajamas, and expertly slid him onto the bed. She transferred the blood bottle from the gurney to the bottle hanger next to the bed, drew the sheet and blanket up over his legs, and asked him if he wanted the head of his bed cranked up.

When he said yes, she cranked him up to a half-seated half-reclining position, gave him a smile, and wheeled the gurney out of the room.

Hutch said, "No access from this window, Captain."

"From this one either," Starsky said.

"Okay," the captain said. "We'll keep two men in the corridor outside and two more in here."

Hutch said, "You don't mean us, do you, Captain?"

"I've got better things than guard duty for you two to do. Soon as Coleman gets off the phone, I'll call in for some uniformed cops."

Coleman was saying into the phone, "So we'll be delayed. It's not that big a deal. I'll get back to you."

He hung up. Captain Dobey started for the phone, but halted to stare at Andrew Mello when the ex-racket king said, "Forget delay. It's over, Coleman."

Everyone else in the room stared at him too.

Mello said, "I'm not testifying."

Dobey said, "You're going to be all right, Andrew. We're going to protect you."

Mello gave a sardonic nod toward Starsky, another toward Hutch. "Starsky and Hutch, your two best men, right? Darrow and Phelps there, too. And still I was hit. Forget it."

The district attorney said, "Mello, Kester tried to hit you. You owe him. You can't let him frighten you."

Mello emitted a disparaging grunt. "Frighten? That isn't it at all, Coleman."

"What, then? Remember, if you refuse to testify, the plea bargain goes down the drain."

"Do your damnedest," Mello said indifferently.

"What's eating you, Andrew?" Dobey asked. "We've always been on opposite sides of the fence, and I've never been one of your admirers, but one thing I gave you was guts."

"It isn't lack of guts, Harold. I'm not thinking about myself."

"Who, then?" Coleman asked.

Mello glanced around at the three police officers, then shook his head. "Not here."

After staring at him for a moment, Starsky said, "You think we're the leak?"

"Somebody is, young man. It's no big deal. When I ran the organization, and Kester was a two-bit bag man, I always, *always* had someone in the police department on my payroll."

Dobey said in an ominous tone, "You're telling me I got someone *now* in my own backyard, leaking information to Kester?"

"How else did it happen? How could Kester know I was at the Red Hart Motel without a leak? How many people did you tell, Coleman?"

"No one," the D.A. said positively. "Not even my wife." After a pause, he amended, "I told Captain Dobey, of course. And Darrow and Phelps knew about it because they took you there."

Mello turned back to Captain Dobey. "And Starsky and Hutch knew. Who else did you tell, Harold?"

Dobey slowly shook his head. "Because we've been suspecting a leak, no one. But there's one other person who knew, Andrew. Your lawyer."

"What reason would Wayne have to fink on me?" Mello inquired. "I pay him big fees."

"Maybe Kester pays him bigger ones," Hutch suggested.

"He *advised* me to testify against Kester," Mello said irritably. "If he was working for Kester, all he would have had to do was advise me not to, and assure me he could beat the Morgan rap. I take his advice."

There didn't seem to be any logical rebuttal to that. The D.A. and the three police officers in the room looked at each other, acutely aware that the possibilities seemed to have narrowed down to them and the two detectives out in the hall.

Captain Dobey said doggedly, "There's no leak in my division."

"How else did it happen, Harold? For thirty years I ran this town, and those are the realities. All you need is the price, and Kester's got it. I'm not risking the life of my—"

He came to an abrupt halt. Dobey said, "The life of who, Andrew?"

Mello merely shook his head.

Don Coleman said, "Mr. Mello obviously doesn't trust the police. Do you trust me, Mello?"

"I can't see you working with Kester. You wouldn't be on my back about testifying before the grand jury if you were."

Glancing from one to the other of the three police officers, Coleman asked, "Would you mind leaving us alone for a few minutes?"

After gazing indignantly from the D.A. to the man in bed and back again, Dobey stalked from the room. Starsky and Hutch followed him out. The captain continued on down the hall to the nurses' station, leaving Starsky and Hutch to stare after him. Darrow and Phelps, still standing in the corridor, gave Starsky and Hutch inquiring looks. Both merely shrugged.

They could see the captain using the phone at the nurses' station. After a time he came back up the hall.

"I have four uniformed cops on the way," he said. "Soon as they get here, you four are relieved of guard duty. Incidentally, Starsky, those two hoods you brought down got away."

"Got away?" Starsky said, surprised. "How?"

"Apparently they had a backup car following them. It scooped them up and scrammed out of the area before the police units got there. A good citizen took down the license number of the backup car, but it turned out to have been stolen only a couple of hours previously."

"How about the motorcycle?" Starsky asked.

"We got it. Registered to a twenty-two-year-old kid named Jonathan Marrs. He's being checked out."

Don Coleman came from the hospital room. When Captain Dobey gave him an inquiring look, he said, "I found out what was bugging him."

"Well?"

Coleman glanced around at the four other policemen before saying, "Didn't you say you wanted two cops on duty inside the room as well as out here?"

Dobey frowned at this evasion of the issue, but he turned to Phelps and Darrow and assigned them the inside duty. As soon as the two detectives had disappeared into the hospital room, Dobey looked at Coleman again.

Taking the captain's arm, the D.A. steered him along the hall a few yards. Starsky and Hutch looked at each other.

"Do you feel slighted?" Starsky asked.

"Like a wallflower who never gets asked to dance," Hutch admitted.

After a conversation lasting some minutes, Captain Dobey briefly returned, leaving the D.A. waiting where he was.

"There's been a development," Dobey said. "Mello asked Coleman not to reveal what he told him to anyone but me. But he didn't stipulate that I couldn't tell anyone. And I *know* neither of you is the leak."

"Thanks, Captain," Hutch said.

"Yeah," Starsky said. "What's the development?"

"It's a little involved, and Coleman's waiting for me to run him back to his office. I'll see you in mine after you're relieved here."

Starsky looked at his watch. "We're on overtime now, Captain. It's twenty-two seconds after five."

Hutch looked at him. "Twenty-two *seconds?*"

"Twenty-seven now," Starsky said.

"It's not all that urgent," Dobey told them. "Report to my office first thing in the morning instead of going out on patrol. And bring along overnight bags. You may be going on a trip."

"Where?" Hutch asked.

"That can hold. Where do you two plan to go for dinner tonight?"

"Is that an invitation?" Hutch inquired.

"No. Just wondered if you might be planning to eat at your buddy's, Huggy Bear."

Starsky and Hutch looked at each other, then back at the captain. Hutch said, "We haven't discussed it, Captain. We haven't even discussed if we're having dinner together. Starsky may have a date. I may decide to get one."

Starsky said, "Why don't you just tell us what's on your mind, Captain?"

"Your buddy seems to know most everything that's going on in the rackets. Maybe he'd know who Kester has working both sides of the street."

"Oh," Starsky said. "We can check that out without necessarily having dinner there." He looked at Hutch. "Okay?"

"Sure," Hutch said. "We can drop by for a beer on the way home."

"One thing, though, Hutch," Starsky said. "I just remembered neither one of us has got a dime. The watch."

"Oh, yes, that damned watch," Hutch said disgustedly. "Sorry, Captain, we couldn't buy a beer."

Captain Dobey took out his wallet. "How much?"

"Twenty should hold us," Starsky said.

Dobey withdrew a ten and two fives and handed them to Starsky.

"Thank you, Captain," Starsky said. "Is this to be regarded as expense money, or a loan?"

"A loan," the captain said. "Repayable in the morning when you report to my office."

Turning, he walked back down the hall to rejoin Coleman, and the two of them continued on to the elevator.

Chapter VIII

THE UNIFORMED POLICEMEN sent to relieve the detectives arrived fifteen minutes later, and Starsky and Hutch got to Huggy Bear's shortly after 5:30. At that time of day the place was packed. Ordinarily Huggy Bear was either table-hopping or tending bar when it was that crowded, but they didn't spot him walking around and a pretty black girl was tending bar.

There were no vacant stools at the bar, but Starsky managed to squeeze between two customers and order two draft beers. As he paid for them, he said to the girl bartender, "Where's Huggy, Dianne?"

"How could you miss him?" she asked. "He's over there in the booth with the bomb."

Starsky backed out with the beers, handed Hutch one, and scanned the booths. He instantly spotted Huggy Bear. He was wearing a garish yellow-and-red plaid suit, a yellow shirt with six-inch-long collar points, and a bright-red bow tie. The stunning black girl across from him was in a skin-tight sheath dress of silver with sequins all over it. The only reason the two detectives had missed the sight was they hadn't expected to see Huggy Bear as a customer.

Following Starsky's gaze, Hutch spotted the pair

too, and blinked. The two detectives moved over to
the booth.

Hutch said, " 'Evening, Huggy."

Looking up, Huggy Bear said, "Hey, you two
shouldn't be comin' in to see me so direct. I mean, at
least mosey around a little. Act casual. Liable to give
my place a bad reputation."

Indicating his beer, Starsky said, "We moseyed.
We're making like regular customers." He smiled at
the girl and she smiled back.

" 'Scuse me," Huggy Bear said. "This is Janet.
Starsky and Hutch, Janet, a couple of buddies despite
being cops."

The gril smiled at Hutch, said, "Hi, Starsky," turned
the smile on Starsky and said, "How are you, Hutch?"

"I'm Starsky," the dark-haired detective said. He
jerked his thumb at Hutch. "He's Hutch."

Hutch said, "See you a minute, Huggy?"

Reluctantly the black man got out of the booth.
"Won't be gone long, honey," he said to the girl.

Hutch steered him over to one of the pinball machines. Starsky gave the girl another smile and followed along. Huggy Bear leaned against the machine.

"Can't you see I'm all tied up with this fine-lookin'
mama?" he asked plaintively.

Starsky said, "Sorry, Huggy, but it won't wait."

"But, man, I got something goin'." His tone turned
slightly resentful. "And I wish you two wouldn't come
on so strong. I don't like to be seen goin' along so
easy in my own joint, man."

"Who'd know?" Starsky asked. "Who'd even recognize you in that rig? You in a parade?" He turned to
Hutch. "Is there a parade in town?"

Hutch shook his head. "I don't know of any parade."

Huggy Bear grinned. "I had to get some conservative threads for the image."

Hutch said, "That's not an image, it's a nightmare.
What's going on?"

Nodding toward Janet, Huggy Bear said, "Well, I

got myself connected with that groovy little chick, see. She's digging me like there's no tomorrow. And you know who she is? *She is* the Treasure Girl!"

The detectives looked at each other inquiringly, realized neither had the faintest idea who the Treasure Girl was, and turned back to Huggy Bear. Starsky said, "The Treasure Girl?"

" 'Bet Your Treasure.' The giveaway show. She's gonna wheel and deal, so I can come on like a contestant—with all the answers. Dig?"

"Yeah," Starsky said, intrigued. "What can you win?"

"All kinds of loot, baby. A trip to the Bahamas, cash, refrigerator, TV set." He paused and his brow furrowed. "Hey, you know where I could fence a TV set?"

"Fence it?" Hutch said. "You mean sell it."

Huggy Bear first looked slightly startled, then enlightened. "Yeah, sell it. That's an idea."

Hutch said, "Sorry to bring you back to earth, Huggy, but we dropped in to talk of other things. Somebody tried to waste Andrew Mello this afternoon."

The black man nodded soberly. "Yeah, I heard."

Starsky said, "It had to be Kester."

Huggy Bear shrugged. "Precisely. So what do you need from me? Kester's got enough hardware to outfit an army. And hit men, all shapes and sizes, local and imported."

"We've got a bigger problem," Hutch said. "Huggy, Kester's got somebody feeding him information."

The black man hiked an eyebrow. "You're losin' me."

Hutch said, "We've got a worm in our apple."

Huggy Bear's lips pantomimed a whistle. "That's heavy."

"Any ideas?" Starsky asked.

Huggy Bear shook his head. "It's not information known among the rank and file, or I'd of heard."

Making a disappointed face, Starsky said, "Ask

around anyway, will you, Huggy? We'll be in touch."

"Yeah, if me and my mama don't go to the Bahamas."

Starsky glanced around the room and said to Hutch, "Want to eat here? Crowded as it is, probably we'd have to wait awhile."

"You didn't pay for your last meal," Huggy Bear said. "You owe me two dollars fifty cents, plus tax of fifteen cents, plus the tip."

"Tip?" Starsky said. "Nobody tips the proprietor of a place."

"I was working as a waiter."

Starsky took out the change from the five-dollar bill he'd used to pay for the beers and counted out two dollars and sixty-five cents into the restaurant owner's outstretched palm. "I am what is known in waiter's jargon as a stiff," he said. "Be glad you got that."

"I am," Huggy Bear assured him. "I thought I was gonna have to waste lots of postage sending bills every month." He returned to his booth.

"Want to wait for a table here?" Starsky asked Hutch.

"Naw, let's pick up a couple of steaks and do them at my place."

"With a herbal salad?" Starsky asked suspiciously.

"Tonight I'll let you make the whole dinner," Hutch said expansively. "No health foods, no organic foods, just whatever you want to make."

"Well, that's more like it," Starsky said, pleased.

But when they got outside, he came to a sudden stop. "Hey, I just talked myself into doing all the work. And I got to buy the steaks too, because you're broke."

"A deal is a deal," Hutch said smugly.

They had been unable to find a parking place nearer than a block away. When they got back to the car, a young uniformed cop was standing on the sidewalk next to it. As Starsky started to unlock the door, the cop said, "If you expect to drive that car instead of having it towed away, mister, I'll have to give you an equipment citation."

With the key in the lock, Starsky looked at him. The cop pointed to the windshield. "Shouldn't be driving with those holes in your windshield. Obstructs your vision."

Taking the key from the lock, Starsky went over to the cop to hold up his ID. After examining it, the policeman said, "Sorry, Officer Starsky. No exceptions."

"A hood put those two holes in there this afternoon," Starsky said. "We were on official police business. I haven't had time to get a new windshield put in yet. Besides, they're both in the center. Windshields used to have a center divider that obstructed vision more than that."

"If there was a divider there, you wouldn't be in violation," the policeman said agreeably. "But rules are rules." He took out his book. "There's no fine involved. You just have to get the slip I give you signed at the garage that fixes your windshield, and turn the slip in at the Traffic Division."

"It'll be fixed by the police garage," Starsky said. "It's an official car."

"Then you can have them sign it," the cop said pleasantly. "May I see your driver's license, please?"

"He doesn't have a license," Hutch said. "It was revoked for drunken driving."

"Aw, come on," Starsky said. "I've had a bad enough day without dumb jokes." He produced his driver's license and handed it to the young cop.

Since they were not going out on patrol in the morning, Starsky and Hutch drove to Parker Center individually instead of one picking the other up, as was their usual custom. Starsky turned the Torino in for repair and left the equipment citation with the mechanic. He took the elevator to the third floor, carrying the overnight bag he had brought along. He found Hutch already in the squad room, seated at one of the long tables with a simple bag on the floor at his feet, and reading the morning paper.

" 'Morning," Hutch said. "Did you see by the papers that we're minor heroes?"

"Yeah. I also saw they published that Mello's at Southern Memorial. So now everybody knows, including Kester."

"He'd have found out anyway," Hutch said philosophically. "Probably has someone on the payroll there, too."

Setting down his bag, Starsky took out his money clip, counted out some bills and handed them to Hutch. "Thanks for the loan."

"You're welcome." Hutch counted the bills, then looked up with a frown. "Hey, there's only eighty-five here. I loaned you ninety."

"Five bucks was your share of the steak and fixin's. I deducted it."

"I thought you were treating."

Starsky said indignantly, "I cooked the damned steaks, made the salad, and grilled the garlic bread. What more did you expect?"

"For you to do the dishes. You left them in the sink."

Starsky held up two fingers. "This isn't the V-for-victory sign," he said. "It's two of these." He folded his index finger, leaving only his middle finger sticking up.

Pushing aside the paper, Hutch stood up. "Same to you, buddy. Let's go see what the captain wants."

They left their bags in the squad room. They found Captain Dobey alone. Starsky paid him the twenty dollars he had borrowed and thanked him for the loan.

"You're welcome," the captain said. "Find out anything from Huggy Bear?"

Starsky shook his head. "He's working on it, though. Anything more on the owner of that motorcycle?"

"Yeah, he has a record. Jonathan 'Dippy' Marrs, three arrests for gambling, one for simple assault. He's a numbers runner, which means he works for Kester, but doesn't necessarily mean Kester knows him. There's hundreds of small-timers in the organization

Kester probably doesn't know. He has a fishy alibi, but a good one."

"Like what?" Hutch asked.

"The girl he lives with claims he's been up in Frisco for a week. She says the motorbike must have been stolen from the garage. She didn't report it because she didn't know it was missing. Says she never looked in there."

"She give a San Francisco address?" Starsky asked.

"Oh, sure. We phoned the S.F.P.D. to check it out. He's there this morning, all right. Fellow who rents the apartment says he's been there for the past six days. Marrs was limping. Told the San Francisco cops he pulled a muscle playing tennis."

"Kester had him flown up in his private plane," Starsky said. "But you'd never prove it."

"No. Nothing on the guy you think you hit. No reports of a wounded man seeking medical attention."

Hutch snorted. "Kester probably has his own medical clinic. What's the development you mentioned, Captain?"

"You two are going to take a trip."

"A vacation?" Starsky asked hopefully. He looked at Hutch. "Because we've been dedicated, loyal, and shot at."

Dobey said, "Hope you didn't bring overnight bags. Yesterday afternoon I didn't know where you were going, and just assumed it would be some distance."

"We brought them," Hutch said.

The captain made a dismissing gesture. "Store them in your lockers. You'll be coming back today. You're only going to Bryland."

"What's Bryland?" Hutch asked.

"A little town outside San Francisco." He threw the switch of his desk intercom. "Terry, bring in those plane tickets and the cash."

"Yes, sir," the civilian secretary's voice said.

Switching off the intercom, Dobey said, "I'll hold the explanation until Coleman gets here. He's overdue now. Mello gave him permission to include you two in his confidence. He had to, since there was no way we could do what Mello wants without you knowing."

Starsky said, "We may as well sit down, then," and sat in one of the chairs next to the wall. Hutch sat next to him.

Chapter IX

THE DOOR OPENED and both Don Coleman and Terry Evers came in. After crisply greeting everyone, the district attorney asked Dobey, "You tell them?"

"Only that they're going to Bryland."

Coleman said to Starsky and Hutch, "The person Mello was concerned about happens to be his daughter. Her name is Joanne Wells. You're being assigned to go up there, pick her up, and bring her back down here. Safe. In one piece."

In an annoyed voice Dobey said, "Coleman, this is my office and these are my men. I think I can explain this detail without any coaching."

Flushing, the D.A. threw the captain an apologetic look.

Captain Dobey glanced up at Terry Evers, who was standing before his desk with a clipboard and three small envelopes in her hands. "Go ahead and get your business done with first, Terry."

"Yes, sir," the girl said.

She went over to hand airline-ticket envelopes to Starsky and Hutch. Holding up the third envelope, she asked, "Who wants to be responsible for the cash expense money?"

Starsky looked at Hutch, who shrugged. "I'll take it," Starsky said.

Terry handed him both the envelope and the clipboard, and also gave him a pen. "You'll have to sign the voucher then."

Signing, Starsky handed back the clipboard and the pen. The secretary left the room.

Captain Dobey said, "Mello has a daughter nobody knew about. He's kept her under wraps, had her live under a different name, so she wouldn't have his. She was educated in Europe, but came back a few years ago. She's the only thing in the world he really cares about."

"And he's afraid Kester might know about her, and grab her to keep him from talking?" Hutch asked.

"Right," Coleman said. "Until she's down here safe—" He paused to glance at Dobey. When the captain nodded permission, he went on, "Until she's with him in a safe house, he won't testify."

Starsky asked, "She know what happened yesterday afternoon?"

The district attorney nodded. "I talked to her on the phone. She's very anxious to see him." He took a slip of paper from his pocket and handed it to Starsky. "Here's the address."

Captain Dobey said, "Given the fact that we may have a leak in this division, this operation is top security. Once you leave this office, you're on your own. You can't call in, you can't ask for help, you can't let anyone know what you're doing or where you are. Is that clear?"

"Clear," Hutch said laconically.

Coleman said, "I want that girl brought here without a scratch."

Starsky gave him a toothy smile. "But you don't mind if we get bruised a little."

The district attorney gave him a quizzical glance. In a dry tone he said, "I understood you gentlemen could take care of yourselves."

Dobey said, "We don't want to attract any attention. When you look at your tickets, you'll see that you're flying from Burbank by PSA instead of from International. When you get to San Francisco, grab a cab over to Bryland, pick her up, and fly her back the same way."

Starsky and Hutch both took their tickets from their envelopes to look at them. Starsky said, "Hey, there's two return tickets in mine."

"Of course," Dobey said. "One's for the girl."

Five men in addition to Harry Kester were gathered in the racketeer's office. Big Curly Dobbs, with his left shoulder bandaged and his arm in a sling, sat on the sofa. Next to him sat Sid Johnson, Kester's second-in-command, a cool, efficient-looking man of forty. The three easy chairs were occupied by Frank Deeks, a quiet, sleepy-looking but also deadly-looking man of forty-five, Terrance (Buck) Buckman, a burly man of about the same age with a low forehead and protruding ears, and William (Willie) Thorn, a pale, slim, rather small man of twenty-six with the eyes of a dead carp. The latter three had varying jobs in the Kester organization, but were also hit men when the need arose.

Kester said, "My ear in the police department couldn't get the girl's address, and there's no Joanne Wells, or Joanne Mello either, listed in the phone book for Bryland. I phoned Dippy Marrs to check. So you're going to have to tail the two cops from the San Francisco airport. They're flying from Burbank at eleven-thirty A.M. Ellie made you four reservations on the eleven A.M. flight from International. Only the four of you are going, because Curly might be more hindrance than asset with that busted wing." He looked at his watch. "It's nearly ten now, so you better get moving. Any questions?"

The sleepy-looking Deeks said, "Starsky and Hutch put me away for eighteen months on a lousy ADW. You got any restrictions on how we handle this?"

"Yes. Don't hurt the girl. She's no good to us dead."

"How about the cops?"

"Make them as dead as you want," Kester said.

The flight from Burbank to San Francisco took an hour and fifteen minutes. Starsky and Hutch lunched on the plane, and disembarked at the San Francisco airport at a quarter to one. There was a line of cabs waiting outside the terminal entrance. The driver of the one they climbed into was a square-bodied, round-headed man of about forty with a cheerful smile and the battered face of an ex-fighter.

"You know where Bryland is?" Starsky asked him.

" 'Course I do. It's a suburb of San Francisco."

"Okay. Take us to 126 Carson Street."

As the cab pulled away, the two detectives studied the cab driver's identification card attached to the back of the front seat. It gave his name as George Shetland.

"You the George Shetland that used to fight middle-weight?" Hutch asked.

"Yeah," the driver said in a pleased voice. "You seen me fight?"

"Once, on television, when I was a kid. But not for long. It was the Kid Kaiser fight."

"Oh, that," George said with a touch of embarrassment. "He caught me with a lucky punch. That was the only time I ever hit the deck in the first round."

"How many times in the second?" Starsky asked.

"A few," the ex-boxer admitted. "But I went ten with Buddy Hooker when he was seventh-place contender."

"How many you win altogether?" Hutch asked.

"Four."

"Out of how many fights?" Starsky asked.

There was a long pause before George said reluctantly, "Eighty-seven."

Bryland was a quiet little town with tree-lined streets. One twenty-six Carson was a huge, two-story brick house that had been converted into a four-unit apartment building. When the two detectives climbed out of the taxi, Hutch told the driver to wait.

Starsky and Hutch both glanced around in all directions, thinking of the leak. Reading each other's minds, they exchanged sheepish glances.

"You too, huh?" Starsky said. "Think we're getting paranoid?"

Hutch shook his head. "I got a funny feeling, and I don't like it. Who the hell can we trust?"

"Like always," Starsky said. "Me and thee."

They climbed steps to the recessed porch of the apartment house. There was an outside door to each apartment, the doors to the lower flats on either side, the ones to the upper flats straight ahead. Starsky took the address slip from his pocket to check the apartment number, and rang the bell to the first-floor flat on the left.

The door opened only as far as a burglar chain would let it, and a pale face peered out. Starsky held his ID up to the crack.

"Just a minute," a pleasantly husky feminine voice said.

She closed the door in order to release the burglar chain, then opened it again, this time all the way. She was an attractive, dark-haired girl in her mid-twenties with a nice figure, about five feet six. She had pale, flawless skin, dark, wide-spaced eyes, and was dressed in a white pantsuit. She gave the two detectives a nervous smile.

"I've been a little cautious about opening the door since I talked to District Attorney Coleman on the phone," she said. "I'm Joanne Mello, better known as Joanne Wells. Come on in."

When they were inside, Starsky said, "I'm Dave Starsky, and this is my partner, Ken Hutchinson, Miss Mello. Or do you prefer Wells?"

"Why don't you make it Joanne?" she suggested.

"Okay," Starsky agreed. "People generally call us Starsky and Hutch."

"I'm still packing," she said. "You can watch me while we talk."

She went into a bedroom and both detectives trailed after her. An open suitcase lay on the bed, and a couple of piles of clothing and some toiletries lay on the bed next to it. Starsky and Hutch stopped just inside the door and watched her load the suitcase.

With her back to them, she asked, "How's my father?"

"He's doing fine," Hutch said. "He's in the hospital under tight security."

"Were you both with him when he was shot?"

"That's right," Starsky said. "We were assigned to protect him."

She looked over her shoulder at him. *"Protect* him?"

Flushing slightly, Starsky said, "He could have been killed, Joanne."

She faced the other way again, long enough to close and latch the suitcase, then turned to face them. After examining them appraisingly for a moment, she said, "Yes, and when I heard about it, I wondered if the police would have liked that."

Hutch's tone didn't show it, but Starsky knew he was holding his temper when he called the girl Miss Mello instead of Joanne. He said, "Look, Miss Mello, what we think of your father has nothing to do with our job. And right now it's getting you back to him in one piece. We intend to do that."

"I asked you to call me Joanne," she said.

Hutch merely shrugged.

After studying him pensively for several seconds, she said in a placating voice, "Look, I'm frightened, and after what happened, I don't feel I can trust anyone. I want to see my father very much, but we've a long way to go." Walking over to a window, she looked out. "And I—I don't know what's out there."

Starsky said, "Neither do we, Joanne. So if you stay close and do what we ask, we'll all get along much better." He went over to lift her suitcase. "We've got a plane to catch."

Going over to a closet, she took out a light coat, but didn't put it on, merely draped it over one arm. She picked up a purse from the dressertop.

"I'm all ready," she said. "How did you get here from the airport? In a rented car?"

"Cab," Hutch said. "It's waiting downstairs."

He preceded her out of the room, not because he was too irritated at her to be courteous, but because it was proper police procedure for one cop to precede a subject who was being guarded, and for the second to bring up the rear.

Chapter X

BECAUSE OF THE difficulty of getting guns past the metal detector at the airport, before the hit team left L.A. Sid Johnson phoned Dippy Marrs in San Francisco from Kester's office. He arranged for Dippy to meet them at the San Francisco airport with three handguns and a sawed-off shotgun. He also arranged for him to have two "clean" cars there, meaning freshly stolen ones from outside San Francisco that the San Francisco police wouldn't yet be looking for.

Johnson drove his own car to International Airport. En route he outlined the strategy to his three henchmen. Its brilliance demonstrated how he had managed to gain the number-two spot in the organization.

"It must be eighteen, twenty miles from the airport to Bryland," he told the three. "You could never in a million years tail a couple of sharp cops like Starsky and Hutch that far without them tumbling. But I been to Bryland, and there's only one road you can take there from the airport. It ain't a freeway, it's an old-fashioned two-laner. We'll pick a spot a little way out-side of town and watch them go by, so we know what kind of car they're in. Then we hit them on the way out, after they've picked up the girl."

Sleepy-looking Frank Deeks, seated in front next to Johnson, asked, "How do we hit them?"

"We box them on a lonely stretch of road about four or five miles out of Bryland." Turning his head slightly to speak to the men in the back seat, he said, "Buck, you'll be driving the lead car, with Thorn riding with you. You'll get ahead of the cops' car. Frank and I will be behind it, with me driving and Frank handling the shotgun. When we reach that lonely stretch, you suddenly slam on your brakes and swing sideways to block the road. We'll close in and Frank will blast them with the shotgun. Then we all hit the dirt and finish them off with handguns, if anybody's left."

Pale young Willie Thorn said, "I thought we weren't supposed to hurt the girl."

"She won't get hurt," Johnson said. "Now we don't know whether they'll be in a taxicab or in a rented car, but in either event I figure one cop will be in the back seat with the girl and the other will be in front. Right?"

"Sounds logical," young Thorn admitted.

"Okay, try to think like a cop for a minute. You're the one in the back seat, and suddenly you realize you're boxed. What do you do?"

After thinking this over, Thorn said, "I shove her down on the floor, then pull my gun."

"Exactly," Johnson said in an approving voice. "The only ones going to get mowed down are those with their heads up, either driving or trying to shoot back. When it's all over, we'll find Mello's daughter nice and safe, hunkered down on the floor of the back seat."

"Hey, that's pretty smart," Thorn said admiringly.

Dippy Marrs, limping slightly, and another twenty-two-year-old youth he introduced only as Ketchup met them at the airport and guided them to a pair of auto-mobiles on the airport parking lot. Both were two-door

sedans a couple years old, one a green Chevrolet, the
other a bright-yellow Ford.

"Shotgun's under the front seat of the Chevy,"
Marrs said. "One handgun's in the glove compartment,
the other two in the glove compartment of the Ford.
All loaded, and with extra ammo."

Johnson nodded approvingly. "What'd they run
you?"

"Hundred fifty for the shotgun, one twenty-five each
for the handguns. Ammo included. Comes to five and
a quarter."

Johnson produced a roll of bills, from which he
peeled seven one-hundred-dollar bills and one fifty.
Handing the money to Marrs, he said, "Hundred each
for you and your buddy, twenty-five for cab fare back
home."

"Gee, thanks," Marrs said.

Johnson drove the green Chevrolet, with Deeks as
his passenger. Buckman drove the Ford, with Willie
Thorn as his copilot. All four examined their weapons
before pulling off the lot. After checking the shotgun,
Deeks set it on the floor between his feet instead of
shoving it back under the seat. The others all shoved
their handguns into their belts.

Leading the way, Johnson found a side road about
a mile outside of Bryland that was perfect for their
purpose. A stand of trees on the left side of the road
obstructed the view into the side road from that direction until vehicles going toward Bryland reached the
intersection, making it extremely unlikely that anyone crossing the intersection on the main road would
notice the two cars parked there. The trees also offered
cover to an observer. Johnson posted Deeks, who
knew Starsky and Hutch better than any of the others,
behind a tree near the edge of the road, from where he
could see the occupants of every passing vehicle from
either direction. Then they all simply waited.

They were in position at 12:45 P.M., about the
time Starsky and Hutch were landing at the airport. It
was forty-five minutes later before Deeks came back

to the green Chevrolet and said to Johnson, "See that Checker Cab that just went by?"

"Yeah. That them?"

"Uh-huh. License 817-LXK."

Climbing from the car, Johnson went back to the yellow Ford parked behind it. Deeks tailed along.

Johnson said to Buckman, "They're in a Checker cab. According to Kester's information, their return-flight reservations aren't until three-thirty, but I figure they'll head back this way soon as they pick up Mello's daughter. Wouldn't be surprised if they passed here on the way back within the next half-hour. I'm going to post Deeks behind that tree again. The road toward Bryland is straight enough here so he should be able to spot the cab coming back a good two hundred yards off. Soon as he does, he'll give you the sign. You take off and make a fast right turn so that you're in front of them. We'll follow as soon as they pass."

"Got it," the man with the protruding ears said. "But if I'm gonna be the lead car, don't you think I ought to pull up in front of you?"

"I was just going to suggest it," Johnson told him.

As Starsky, Hutch, and the girl started down the steps to the street, the driver got out of the taxi to open the trunk. Starsky deposited the suitcase and Joanne's coat in the trunk as Hutch held open the rear door for the girl to get in. He got in back with her, and Starsky got in front with the driver.

"Back to the airport," Starsky directed.

As they pulled away, the girl nodded toward the driver and whispered to Hutch, "Is he a policeman in disguise too?"

Hutch shook his head. "An ex-boxer. Name is George."

George hadn't heard the whisper, but he heard Hutch's remark. "Pleased to meet you, miss," he said.

Looking slightly startled, she said politely, "How are you, George?"

After that there was silence until they neared the

edge of town, but the girl suddenly broke it by saying to Hutch, "I'm sorry for what I said about the police and my father. Okay?"

"Okay," he said. "Apology accepted."

"And I do understand what your feelings toward him must be."

"Let's just say your father is not one of our favorite people," Hutch said. "But that doesn't affect our attitude toward his safety. We and two other policemen nearly got wasted saving his skin yesterday."

"But you don't really know him," she said in an earnest voice.

Turning sidewise in his seat, Starsky said over his shoulder, "Lady, I know your father inside out. I know what he did to send you to that fancy European college, and to buy you fifteen-thousand-dollar cars."

In a warning tone Hutch said. "Starsk."

Starsky faced front again. There was a long silence. Again it was the girl who finally broke it.

In a muffled voice she said, "My father's occupation —business—whatever you want to call it—I was never part of it. He kept our lives separate. He was good to me. He loved me very much. And when I eventually found out, I thought I never wanted to see him again. I was glad my name was different. But he's an old man now. He's trying to make up for what he's done."

Obviously the girl was unaware of her father's motive for testifying before the grand jury. Again turning sidewise in his seat, Starsky said, "Make up, hell. He's copping—"

"Starsk!" Hutch interrupted.

Glancing at him, Starsky subsided. Hutch said equably, "She's got a point."

Sighing, Starsky went along with his partner's desire not to upset the girl any more than necessary. "Yeah, Joanne, maybe leopards can change spots after all."

He faced front again. There was little traffic on the road, and there had been none in their lane since they left Bryland, but up ahead a yellow Ford sedan came from a side road and turned in the same direction they were going.

Starsky said to George, "How far is the airport from Bryland?"

"About eighteen miles. Sixteen from here, maybe. Hey, you guys sound like cops."

"We are," Starsky said. He pointed to the speedometer. "Move it, George."

George bore down slightly on the accelerator. To himself he muttered aloud, "Funny, they don't look like cops."

As the distance between the taxi and the yellow Ford ahead began to decrease, the Ford picked up speed to widen it back to the same interval. "One of those guys can't stand to be passed," George muttered, again to himself but again out loud.

They were now entering open country, a stretch of planted fields. Off to their left about a quarter mile they could see another road paralleling theirs, but it was gravel. The two roads were connected at intervals by other gravel roads and by rough dirt roads.

Hutch had positioned himself in the rear seat so that he could see into the taxi's side-view mirror. He spotted the green Chevrolet behind them the moment it appeared in the mirror. Leaning forward, he tapped Starsky's shoulder.

"Green Chevy," he said when Starsky turned in his seat.

Peering back through the rear window, Starsky said, "Yeah."

"Something wrong?" the driver inquired.

"Probably not," Starsky said, still looking back. "Just watching the green Chevy back there. Could be tailing us."

George looked in the rearview mirror. After examining the car about fifty yards behind them for some time, he said in a light tone that failed to mask his uneasiness, "Tailing us? Hey, come on. Lotsa people go to the airport, and this is the only road there. Where else can you catch a plane? Right?"

"Right," Starsky agreed.

"I mean, we been following that yellow car up ahead, and are *they* worried?"

Starsky turned to look at the car ahead. It began to slow down. He looked back again to see the green Chevy suddenly pick up speed and start to overtake them.

"What do you think, Hutch?" he asked.

Hutch studied the slowing yellow Ford ahead, glanced into the side-view mirror, and suddenly clamped the fingers of his right hand around the back of Joanne's neck to hurl her face down on the floor.

"It's a squeeze!" he said.

Chapter XI

JUST AS IT reached one of the dirt tracks connecting the paved road with the parallel gravel one off to the left, the yellow Ford suddenly broadsided to a halt, blocking both lanes of the main thoroughfare as well as access to the dirt crossroad. Behind the cab the green Chevrolet surged forward.

Before George could react, Starsky slid over in the seat, slammed his left foot on the brake pedal, and twisted the steering wheel to the right. The cab skidded sideways with the front wheels in the dry dirt of the shoulder, raising a cloud of dust that momentarily acted as a smokescreen. It came to a halt with the front wheels at the lip of a deep ditch running alongside the dirt side road.

Starsky tumbled out with his gun drawn, and fell flat to the ground when he saw the shotgun barrel pointing at him from the right front window of the green Chevrolet bearing down on him. The shotgun roared, the blast taking out the right rear side window of the cab.

Rising on his elbows, Starsky fired a microsecond later, aiming at the Ford's driver. From the hole appearing in the windshield, Starsky could tell that the slug caught the man high in the center of the chest. The Chevy careened out of control to swing left across the shoulder into a plowed field.

Meantime Hutch had tumbled out the other side of the cab, slamming the door behind him to protect the girl huddled on the floor. He was on one knee, aiming his gun in the direction of the yellow Ford when the shotgun blast ripped out the side window.

A heavyset man with a low forehead and protruding ears and a slim younger man had both erupted from the Ford with guns in their hands. They fired at Hutch at the same instant he fired at the younger man. He heard the slugs slam into the side of the cab on either side of him. Hutch's slug caught the slim man in the left thigh, and he went down.

Before the heavyset man could fire again, Starsky jumped out from the other side of the cab and threw a quick shot at him. It missed, but it made the man dive for cover behind the Ford.

The man with the shotgun, momentarily stunned but now recovered, rolled from the front seat of the mired-down Chevrolet. Dropping to one knee, he fired an instant after Starsky had spotted him from the corner of his eye and had dropped flat.

This time the shotgun blast ripped out the rear window of the taxi. The cabdriver was in the act of throwing himself out the right-hand front door, left open by Starsky. Pitching face down to hug the ground, he gasped to himself, "What the hell is going on?"

Starsky fired at the man with the shotgun, driving him behind the green Chevy, then raced behind Hutch to jerk open the left front door of the cab and throw himself under the steering wheel.

"Get in!" he yelled. "Everybody stay down and hang on!"

George scrambled back into the front seat as a passenger, and slammed the door. Hutch put a slug in the side of the yellow Ford to make the wounded man hug the ground and keep the heavyset man down, then jerked open the rear door and jumped in to crouch on his knees on the rear seat, leaving the whole floor to the girl.

As Hutch slammed the rear door, Starsky rammed the car into reverse, gunned the engine, and twisted the wheel to the right. When the cab had roared backward about fifty feet, he braked to a screeching halt, shifted into low, and gunned forward. He veered left onto the dirt shoulder at the left-hand side of the road and floored the accelerator. Leaning out the shattered side window, Hutch slammed two more shots into the yellow Ford to discourage any fire from that direction.

The ditch bordering the dirt side road continued on the left side of the main road, too, and it was just as deep and just as wide there. There was a slight rise at its edge, though, just enough to give the cab a little lift. The cab soared across the ditch to land on the near side of the dirt road and skid toward the ditch on the other side. When Starsky jammed on the brakes and spun the wheel left, it skidded sideways to the very edge of the other ditch, but not quite over into it. He floored the accelerator again, shifted from *low* into *drive* and roared along the dirt road in the direction of the gravel road paralleling the main one.

Hutch kept the heads of their assailants down by emptying his gun at the other two cars through the glassless rear window. Then they were out of effective range. Ejecting the empty shells, Hutch quickly reloaded. He put away his gun before helping the cowering girl back up onto the seat.

"Watch the broken glass," he said solicitously. "Careful where you sit."

"Jesus!" George breathed. "Where'd you learn to drive? On a midget auto racecourse?"

Behind them the gunmen were having problems. Frank Deeks peered in at Johnson, saw he was dead, then looked at the wheels of the Chevrolet. They were buried to the hubcaps in the loose dirt of the plowed field. Abandoning the car as hopeless, he waded through the loose dirt to the road, then ran over to where Buck Buckman was bending over the wounded Willie Thorn, who was now sitting up.

"It's only a flesh wound, I think," the pale young man said hopefully. "Can you help me into the car?"

Cars coming simultaneously from both directions braked to a halt at that moment. Deeks quickly tossed his shotgun to the floor of the Ford's rear seat through the already open front door, and bent the front seat forward. The other two shoved their guns into their belts. The occupants of the two halted cars stared from them to the mired-down Chevrolet, but the sight of the guns discouraged anyone from investigating. Deeks and Buckman ignored both cars as they helped the wounded man into the back seat.

"What about Johnson?" Buckman asked.

"Dead," Deeks said briefly.

He climbed in back with Thorn. Buckman slid under the steering wheel, started the engine, and gunned forward. They were already headed in the right direction. The country was flat enough here so that they could see the gravel road winding through it for some distance. A thin cloud of dust, rapidly settling, showed the direction taken by the taxicab, but the cab had enough of a lead to be out of sight now. At the gravel road Buckman turned right and began to raise his own cloud of dust.

In the back seat Thorn had pulled down his trousers and Deeks was examining his wound. "No exit wound, so it's still in there," he said. "But it didn't cut any veins or arteries, or you'd be bleeding more. We can fix it up to hold you until we get back to Los Angeles."

He took out a handkerchief that was already folded into a small square, placed it over the wound, stripped off his necktie and used it to tie the handkerchief in place.

"Okay, pull up your pants," he said.

Thorn pulled up his trousers. Aside from a small hole in the cloth of the left leg, surrounded by a slightly larger circle of blood, there was no external evidence of his wound.

Buck Buckman said, "Those two cops are a little hard to put down, aren't they?"

"Yeah," Deeks said. "But it's gonna be a pleasure to do it."

A good three miles ahead of the Ford, Starsky braked to a halt at the entrance of a lane leading to a farmhouse. He said to George, "You can probably find a phone in there to call yourself a taxi. Get out."

"What do you mean, get out?" George asked indignantly. "This is *my* cab."

"You'll get paid later," Starsky said with impatience. "Repair bill and all. We'll see to it."

Leaning over the back of the seat, Hutch grabbed Starsky's left arm. "Give him your watch for security."

"No way!" Starsky said, jerking loose his arm.

Hutch grabbed it again, slid a thumb beneath the expansion band and jerked the watch from his wrist. He handed it to George, who accepted it doubtfully.

"This is a terrific watch," Hutch said. "Worth fifteen-hundred dollars. Or, at rock bottom, at least three-sixty."

"I can't drive a watch," George said in a high voice.

Starsky said, "What do you mean, terrific? You said you hated that watch."

"Not any more," Hutch said.

Leaning over the seat, he reached past George to open the right front door, shoved the ex-boxer out and pulled the door closed. "You'll be safer without us," he said. "Contact the Los Angeles police for your reward."

"The Los Angeles police!" George yelled after them as the taxi roared off. "That's four hundred and fifty miles from here!"

But the cab was already two hundred yards beyond, obscured by a wake of dust cloud. George examined the watch, studied the back with puzzlement, then shrugged and slipped it on his wrist. He started to walk up the lane.

He was inside, making his phone call, when through a window he saw the yellow Ford speed by, raising another cloud of dust.

Hutch examined the girl seated beside him. Her face was pale, but otherwise she seemed pretty well in control of herself.

"Are you all right?" he asked.

"Psychologically," she said. "I think I'm sitting on a piece of glass."

Gripping the back of the front seat, she raised herself up. Hutch took out his handkerchief, raised himself also, and brushed the whole seat clean. Peering, he said, "A sliver's stuck to the seat of your pants."

"Well, get it," she said.

He flicked it away with the handkerchief.

They both sat back down. The road began a long, sweeping curve that rapidly increased the distance between it and the main road, and eventually headed them due south instead of in the westerly direction they had been traveling.

"Where are we going?" Hutch asked.

"Not back to the airport," Starsky said. "That'll be the first place they look."

"We're heading south. Why not just keep driving?"

Starsky said, "Where does this road go, Joanne?"

"To Jenson's Corners, then connects with a freeway. You mean you're going to drive all the way?"

"We really don't have much choice," Hutch said.

"But four hundred and fifty miles! Shouldn't we call a sheriff or something? I mean, why don't we get a police escort?"

"What do you think we are?" Starsky asked.

Hutch said, "It's probably safer if we don't give away our location."

"Give away our location?" the girl said in a puzzled tone. "But what difference would it make? They already know."

Looking in the rearview mirror, Starsky said, "Not necessarily. They're not behind us. Maybe they assumed we'd cut back to the main road and continue on toward the airport."

"How can you see anything in the rearview mirror with all the dust you're raising?" Joanne asked.

Hutch turned around to peer through the rear window. He said, "I can see the road for a long way back before we hit that curve. And I don't see any dust cloud following us."

They rode on in silence for some minutes. Finally the girl said, "Something I don't understand. Over the phone Mr. Coleman told me what my father was afraid of was that Kester would try to kidnap me. But those men tried to kill me."

"That's been bothering me too," Hutch said. "What do you think, Starsk?"

Starsky made no immediate reply, thinking it over. Eventually he said, "Maybe they just gave us credit for being good cops. She didn't get hurt, did she? Maybe they figured we'd push her down on the floor, so they could burn us without hurting her."

The girl looked at Hutch. "I haven't thanked you," she said. "I guess you did save my life."

About ten miles farther on they came to a small village.

"This Jenson's Corners?" Starsky asked.

"No," the girl said. "Farther on."

He continued on through the village.

Chapter XII

WHEN THE YELLOW Ford reached the point where the gravel road began to curve south, Buckman slowed, pulled over onto the shoulder, and parked.

"This thing don't go to the airport," he said. "They must of cut back to the main road somewhere."

"Some car just passed here," Frank Deeks disagreed. "And there ain't so much traffic on this road that it'd likely be anybody else."

"How do you know some car just passed here?"

"There's still a little dust haze in the air."

"I don't see it," Buckman said.

"Me neither," Thorn put in.

Deeks was seated on the left side of the back seat. Climbing past the wounded Thorn, he pulled forward the front seat and got out on the right. Stooping, he examined the roadside vegetation, running a finger over the leaves of several bushes.

Getting back into the car, but this time in front, Deeks said, "There's fresh dust settled on the leaves alongside the road. They passed here."

"How you know it's fresh dust?" Buckman inquired. "You some kind of Indian scout?"

"I'm part Indian," Deeks said. "And I grew up in Oregon."

Buckman tugged at one of his protruding ears as he considered these two statements. He got a mental picture of Deeks as a young brave following a forest trail, accompanied by an ancient Indian who pointed

out bent twigs and places where grass had been
crushed by passing feet.

"You think they took the road south, huh?" he said.

"I think it's worth a chance. What if they did go to
the airport? How we going to take them there, with
a million people around? But if they took this route,
we could catch 'em somewhere isolated."

"Odds seem to favor this way," Thorn agreed from
the back seat.

"Okay," Buckman said, starting up again. "But
we're running low on gas."

"Stop at the first place you see and fill up," Deeks
suggested.

That was ten miles farther on, in a crossroads village. As the attendant checked the oil, Buckman asked
him where the gravel road went.

"Jenson's Corners," the man said. "About a hundred and fifty miles. Nothing much in between but a
few ranger stations."

"Where from Jenson's Corners?"

"Ten miles beyond you hit a cutoff to Highway
101."

As they drove out of the village, Buckman asked
Deeks, "Where in Oregon you from?"

"Salem."

Buckman glanced sidewise at him. "You grew up
in a forest in Salem?"

"Who said I grew up in a forest?"

"Well, you pulled all that malarkey about being
able to cut sign."

"Oh, that," Deeks said. "I see a lot of Western mov-
ies."

When the odometer showed they had driven fifty
miles on the gravel road since passing through the
little village, which had been the last sign of civiliza-
tion they saw, Starsky asked, "How far is this Jenson's Corners?"

"About a hundred more miles," Joanne said.

"A hundred miles! On this gravel road?"

"You hit blacktop within another ten miles," the girl told him.

"I hope we also hit a gas station," Starsky muttered.

"Not before Jenson's Corners," she said.

"Judas Priest!" he exploded. "Why didn't you tell me that when we passed through that village back there?"

"You didn't ask me."

"Well, I hope we make it," Starsky said dourly. "We've got a little over a quarter tank."

A little farther on Starsky complained, "This cab has no dash clock. You wearing your watch today, Hutch?"

"Uh-huh. Three thirty-seven, four seconds, and one tick."

"Very funny," Starsky said. "What's the phase of the moon?"

"What are you two talking about?" the girl asked.

"It's a long story having to do with three hundred and sixty dollars," Hutch told her.

When they reached the blacktop road, they began to climb into mountainous country. The road became progressively more winding and hilly, and the surrounding countryside became progressively less inhabited. Starsky had to drive at forty or under most of the time because of the sharp curves.

About 4:30 Starsky said, "You know we haven't passed a crossroad since we hit this blacktop?"

"We won't before Jenson's Corners," Joanne said. "There aren't any. There's no way you could change your mind now, because there's nowhere else to go."

"Hope our gas holds out that long," Starsky said. "The gauge is down to one-eighth."

"How much farther we got to go?" Hutch asked.

Starsky looked at the odometer. "About sixty miles, if Joanne was right when she said it was about a hundred."

"That's cheerful news," Hutch said. "You can't have more than three gallons left. We better hope you're getting twenty miles to the gallon."

About forty miles farther on the road ran straight across a wide valley to a mountain. As they topped the crest of the rise just before it and started down, they could see the road stretching ahead for at least five miles, descending to the floor of the valley, running along level for a time, then climbing again until it disappeared from view over the distant crest.

They were halfway up the far side when Hutch, who had been periodically looking back during the entire ride, said, "Oh-oh."

The girl turned to look back. Starsky asked, "What's the matter?"

Hutch said, "A yellow Ford sedan just came over the crest of the hill behind us."

Because of the upward slant of the road, Starsky couldn't see the car in the rearview mirror. "Is it them?" he asked.

"Too far back to tell," Hutch said. "Must be three miles, at least. But if it is, they've spotted us too. How's the gas holding out?"

"It registered empty when we started down the hill. I didn't want to upset anybody by mentioning it."

"Then why are you upsetting us now?" Hutch asked.

Joanne said hopefully, "Maybe the gauge isn't accurate. I had a car once that ran out of gas when the gauge showed one-eighth full."

"That's an encouraging note," Starsky said dryly.

When they got out of the valley, the road became winding and hilly again. Starsky drove as fast as he dared, trying to put distance between them and the pursuing yellow Ford.

They were nearing the top of a grade when the engine began to sputter. The car started to falter just short of the crest, then the engine took hold again and they made it over. Two miles beyond, downhill all the way, they could see Jenson's Corners. There were only four buildings and a house trailer, but one of the buildings was a garage with gas pumps in front of it.

"Hardly Los Angeles," Starsky said. "But it's the nicest-looking town I ever saw."

Shifting into *neutral,* he let the cab coast. The road was relatively straight all the way, because the village nestled in the bottom of a small valley, but there were two moderately sharp curves. Starsky negotiated both without braking by cutting clear over onto the shoulder on the wrong side of the road as he reached them. But even then the cab came perilously close to overturning as they screamed around the bends, both times the right wheels going off onto the shoulder in the middle of the curves.

As they roared into the village, Starsky shifted back into gear and slowed. There was still a little gas in the tank, apparently. He pulled up to the servicestation pumps, then changed his mind, circled the place, and pulled in close behind the garage.

"Maybe they'll go right on by," he said.

Inside the garage sixty-year-old Abel Jenson was working on the engine of his 1950 Plymouth when a bell indicated that a vehicle had pulled in next to the pumps. Wiping his hands on a greasy cloth, he went to wait on the customer. He was a lean, slightly stooped, weary-looking man in grease-stained coveralls.

To his surprise, there was no car at the pumps. He looked around in all directions, sure that he had heard the bell ding, but no vehicle was in sight. He was returning to the garage when he heard the sound of a car engine off in the distance to the north, and looked that way to see a yellow Ford sedan coming down the two-mile grade. He waited, assuming the car would stop for gas, since most cars passing through Jenson's Corners did. But it went right on through town at high speed, climbed the south grade, and disappeared.

Jenson started to return to the garage a second time, but halted again when a Checker cab circled from behind the garage and pulled up at the pumps. With a slightly startled expression on his face, he went over to the cab as all three occupants climbed out.

"Fill it, okay?" Starsky said. "Regular."

Jenson looked at the glassless side and rear windows and at the pocks in the paint where shotgun pellets had hit the cab. "Have a little accident?" he asked.

"Actually it was on purpose," Starsky said.

As Jenson thrust the gas nozzle into the tank vent, the two detectives and the girl glanced around. The building housing the repair garage and the service-station office also had a section that seemed to be living quarters, they noted, because there were faded curtains at the windows. A number of old cars were parked around the station, one of them a battered mobile van. Next to the station was a square brown stucco building with a sign in front of it saying EATS. Across the street there was a general store with a house trailer next to it, presumably where the store's proprietor lived, and a seedy-looking motel with only six units. Four of the units had automobiles parked in front of them.

Starsky looked up at the grade climbing from the south end of the valley. "Must be five miles past here by now, way they were highballing."

Hutch looked that way too. After a moment he said thoughtfully, "They see a lot of empty road ahead of them, they're liable to turn around. We better lay back a little, see what they do."

After considering this, Starsky turned to Jenson and said, "When you're through filling it, could you park it inside, close the door and forget you saw it?"

The service-station proprietor hung up the hose, replaced the gas cap and said, "Eleven dollars and twenty cents."

Starsky paid him with a twenty. As the man handed him the change, he said, "Well?"

"Why would I do a thing like that?" Jenson asked.

Pulling more bills from his pocket, Starsky handed a ten to the man. "How many guesses do I get?"

"I mean, I don't know you."

Handing him another bill, Starsky said, "What's in a name?"

"Or what you're up to."

"I'm up to thirty dollars," Starsky said, holding out a third bill.

Jenson tried to take it, but this time Starsky held on.

"Deal," he said finally.

Starsky released his hold on the bill and Jenson hurriedly pocketed all three bills.

Chapter XIII

STARSKY ASKED HUTCH what time it was, and Hutch told him it was a couple of minutes before six P.M.

"It will be midnight before we get to Los Angeles," Joanne said.

Starsky shrugged. "It stays light until nine P.M. this time of year, so we'll only have three hours' night driving. Anybody getting hungry?"

"I am," the girl said. She turned to the service-station proprietor. "How's the food next door?"

"Probably won't kill you," he said.

She looked from Starsky to Hutch. Both shrugged philosophically. Cops eat at so many greasy spoons in the course of their work that they tend to develop a tolerance to bad food.

Hutch said, "We can keep an eye on the road from in there."

They started toward the restaurant, but halted again when the service-station proprietor said in after-thought, "Except maybe for the meat loaf."

They considered this, then continued on. They had to pass the mobile van to get to the restaurant. Starsky paused momentarily to look it over, then hurried after the others.

The dining room was long and narrow, with a counter running along the right side and with a half-dozen booths against the wall on the left side. There was no room between the counter and the booths for additional tables. At the near end of the counter was a grill and a steam table. Behind them was a swinging door into the kitchen.

Three of the booths were occupied by middle-aged couples, presumably from the motel across the road. A tall, skinny man of about forty with Bugs Bunny teeth seemed to be both cook and waiter. He wore an apron and a chef's cap, but at the moment was delivering two plates of bacon and eggs to one of the booths.

They waited until the waiter-cook went back behind the counter and approached them. Giving them a rabbit grin, he asked, "Help you?"

"What's good tonight?" Starsky asked.

"The hot plate is meat loaf." He indicated a grayish mound in a pan on the steam table.

After gazing at it, Hutch asked, "How about sandwiches?"

"Jelly, baloney. Or I can make you a meat-loaf sandwich."

Starsky said, "You're pushing the meat loaf awful hard."

"We got a mess of it," the cook said. He turned back to Hutch. "Or bacon and eggs."

Hutch and the girl both looked over at the booths. All three couples had plates of bacon and eggs before them. No one was eating very heartily, and two of the women weren't eating at all. The eggs were floating in grease.

Turning back to the cook, Hutch said, "Just coffee."

"Two," Joanne said.

She and Hutch moved over to the booth nearest the front window. Hutch took the seat facing the window, so that he could see the road. She sat opposite him.

"I'll try the meat loaf," Starsky decided.

The cook looked surprised but gratified. Starsky went over to the booth and sat next to the girl.

Hutch said to the girl, "You handled yourself pretty well. Most women would have been hysterical by now."

Flushing slightly, she said, "Thank you." After a pause, she said, "I wonder how my father is?"

"He's a tough old turkey," Starsky assured her. "He won't quit."

The cook brought over two coffee mugs and set them before Hutch and the girl. Going back behind the counter, he returned with Starsky's meal. There was a slab of meat loaf with gravy over it, a scoop of lumpy mashed potatoes with more gravy, some peas, and a slice of buttered bread.

Joanne had just tasted the coffee. "How old is this?" she asked the cook.

"I made it fresh yesterday. Anything else?"

"Glass of water," Starsky suggested.

"Oh, sure."

He went away again and returned with a glass of water. While he was gone, Joanne poured a lot of cream substitute into her coffee from a pitcher on the table. When she stirred it, its color became as gray as Starsky's meat loaf before it was disguised with gravy. Hutch decided to leave his black.

When the waiter left again, the girl said to Hutch, "You said it was safer not to give our location away. Why?"

"Harry Kester has somebody planted in the department. When he tried to kill your father, he knew when and where to make the hit. Those men we just lost, they weren't on our tail by accident. Someone told them where to pick us up."

The girl frowned. "So we're targets, and we can't even ask for help?"

Between mouthfuls of food Starsky said, "That's about the way it is."

They both watched Starsky eat for a time. Obviously he was enjoying his meal, and was particularly en-

joying the meat loaf. Intrigued, Hutch finally took his
coffee spoon, scooped up a tiny taste of it from
Starsky's plate, and put it in his mouth. His face assumed a strange expression.

Setting down the spoon, he said, "That's awful!"

"I thought it was pretty good," Starsky said.

He cleaned his plate, got up, and carried it over to
the counter.

"Yes?" the cook asked.

"Could I have some more? Just the meat loaf."

"You like it?" the cook said in a startled voice.
"You really like it?"

"It's the special, isn't it?"

Avoiding an answer, the cook carried the plate to
the steam table. Starsky started back for the booth.
But as he reached it, through the front window he
caught sight of the yellow Ford cruising back into
town.

"Oh-oh," he said. "Hutch."

Hutch looked that way, and Joanne turned in her
seat to look also.

They watched the Ford pull up before the pumps
of the service station. The three occupants got out
of the car. The youngest one was limping.

"Know who that sleepy-looking guy is, Hutch?"
Starsky asked. "I didn't get a good look at him when
he was blasting that shotgun at us, but that's Frank
Deeks. We put him away for two-to-five on an ADW.
I think he served eighteen months."

"I know all of them," Hutch said. "But in all the
excitement, I didn't recognize them either. The guy
with the low forehead and jug ears is Buck Buckman.
The kid who's limping because I put a bullet in his
leg is Willie Thorn. Both Kester hit men."

"What's an ADW?" the girl asked.

"Assault with a deadly weapon," Starsky informed
her. "In this case the deadly weapon was his fist. He
crippled a guy."

From where they were, they couldn't see the repair

garage, but they could see that the Checker cab had been moved.

"Hope that guy running the station had enough sense to close the garage door," Starsky said.

"If he hadn't, they'd be checking it out," Hutch assured him. "They all looked around in all directions, including that way, and they don't seem to have spotted anything that interested them."

The service-station proprietor came into their range of vision. Deeks said something to him, and the man shrugged, shook his head. Deeks said something else, and the proprietor moved to the pump to put gasoline in the Ford. The three hit men conferred. They looked toward the restaurant, then across the road toward the general store and the motel. Deeks started across the road, Buckman and Thorn headed for the restaurant.

"What are we going to do?" Joanne asked in a scared voice.

"Come on," Hutch said.

Taking her hand, he led her behind the counter and toward the door into the kitchen. Over his shoulder he said to Starsky, "Pay the man—and get that table cleared!"

Starsky picked up the two coffee cups in one hand, and the glass of water in the other. They were difficult to handle because all three were nearly full. He thought for a moment, set them down again, took out a twenty-dollar bill and clamped it in his teeth. Picking up the cups and the glass once more, he ran over to the counter to hold them out to the cook.

The cook was standing open-mouthed, a plate of meat loaf in his hand, gazing at the kitchen door through which Hutch and the girl had disappeared. Starsky continued to hold out the cups and the water glass to him, at the same time thrusting forward his jaw with the bill clamped in his teeth.

"Heep va ksange," he said indistinctly.

The startled cook took only a second to decide which burden to relieve Starsky of first. He chose the money. Giving up, Starsky set down the cups and glass on the counter.

As he hurried behind the counter and headed for the door through which Hutch and Joanne had disappeared, he snarled, "Get that stuff out of sight. That twenty is to make you forget you saw us when those guys coming in ask. If you remember, I'll come back and pull your cork."

Starsky passed through the kitchen and exited by a door at the rear of the building. Hutch and Joanne were already outside. Hutch was peering around the edge of the building.

Straightening, Hutch said, "Okay, they've gone into the restaurant."

Taking the girl's hand again, he quickly crossed the open space between the restaurant and the service station to the area behind the garage. Starsky followed. The garage had a back door, closed. Opening it, Hutch led the way in. The wide front door, which rolled up and down, was closed.

There were three bays in the garage. One contained a 1950 Plymouth with a torn-down engine. Another contained the Checker cab. The third was empty.

There was a door from the garage into the service-station office, also closed. Opening it, Hutch peered in. The proprietor was seated at a desk. When he looked around nervously, Hutch crooked a finger at him.

Getting up, the man came over to the door. He said, "Hey, listen, those fellows out there, they're looking for you. Maybe you ought to tell me who you are, and what's going on."

Hutch showed the man his ID.

"You're the fuzz?" the man said in surprise.

Starsky and Hutch exchanged amused glances. Looking slightly embarrassed, the service-station proprietor said, "I heard that on TV."

"God bless TV," Starsky said.

Hutch took the man by the arm, drew him into the garage, and closed the door into the office. "What's your name?" he asked.

"Jenson. Abel Jenson."

"This town is named after you?" Starsky asked.

"My grandfather," Jenson said, then added unnecessarily, "he's dead."

Hutch said, "Listen, Abel, we want to borrow that mobile van you have parked outside. We'll leave the cab as security."

Jenson considered this dubiously. "If you're the police, where'd you get the cab?"

Nodding toward Starsky, Hutch said, "We traded it for his watch."

Jenson's eyes widened. "That must have been some watch."

"It cost three hundred and sixty bucks," Starsky said. He turned to Hutch. "And I ain't gonna get it back with no funky mobile van."

"We'll settle it all later," Hutch said. "We got a deal?" he asked the service-station proprietor.

The man shrugged. "Sure, I'm a citizen. I believe in law and order. And personal enterprise. You can borrow the van for two hundred."

"Two hundred!" Starsky said.

"Well, I gotta give some to the guy who owns it."

"Pay him," Hutch said to Starsky.

Chapter XIV

STARSKY TOOK OUT his money clip and counted out four fifty-dollar bills. Examining what he had left, he said, "Expense money's running kind of low."

As Jenson pocketed the bills, Hutch held out his hand, palm up. "Keys?"

"There ain't none. Just twist the wires under the dash. Want gas?"

"Cars run better that way."

"I filled it this morning," Jenson said. "Be another ten."

After gazing at the man for a moment, Hutch said to Starsky, "Pay the man."

Taking the girl's arm, Hutch steered her out the back door. Starsky gave the service-station proprietor another ten.

At the back door Starsky turned to give Jenson some parting advice. "If I were you, I'd disappear till those guys leave."

When the back door closed behind the detective, Abel Jenson stood considering this for a time, but it was a very short time. Also exiting by the back door, he headed for the apple orchard behind the service station and the restaurant.

Hutch was peering around the corner of the building toward the front. Starsky and Joanne watched the coveralled Jenson hurry toward the orchard and disappear among the trees.

"Where's he going?" she asked.

"Taking my advice."

Turning around, Hutch said, "All clear at the moment."

Starsky said, "You two wait here until you hear the engine catch, then haul out."

Quickly he moved over to the van and opened the back door so that Hutch and the girl could get in fast. Then he moved around to the driver's side of the cab. When he gripped the handle, the door opened only about an inch. Peering through the glass, he saw that it was roped shut on the inside. Apparently the latch was broken.

Starsky moved around to the other door, but before he reached it, he heard Buck Buckman's voice say, "They couldn't disappear into thin air. Not thin air."

The voice came from in front of the restaurant. There was no time for Starsky to open the cab door an jump in. There was no time to run back behind the garage. Starsky dropped flat, rolled over on his back and slid everything but his legs beneath the van.

Turning his head sidewise, Starsky saw two pairs of legs appear, one limping. The legs halted, and turned toward him. They didn't approach, however. They just remained there. Starsky realized they were examining his legs sticking out from under the van. He was thankful that he was wearing faded Levi's. If it had been Hutch under there, his impeccably pressed slacks and highly polished shoes would instantly have given away that it was no mechanic.

If he just lay there, they probably would come over to investigate anyway, Starsky realized when the legs failed to move on. Frantically he felt the ground on both sides of him, running his palms over all the area he could reach. His right hand brushed against a baseball-sized rock. Picking it up, he began to pound on the muffler.

The legs moved on to stop in front of the yellow Ford. Since they were still visible to him there, Starsky knew the van was still in their view. He decided to stay where he was for the moment, but he stopped pounding.

Behind the garage Hutch and Joanne heard Buckman's remark, followed by a period of silence. Hutch started to peer around the corner, but quickly drew back when he spotted Buckman and Thorn facing that way. They didn't see his face momentarily appear because their attention was focused on the van.

Drawing his gun, Hutch dropped face down, edged to the corner on his elbows, and peered around it at ground level. Buckman and Thorn were still looking at the van. At that moment a pounding noise came from it, and Hutch glanced that way and saw Starsky lying on his back beneath it. The pounding seemed to convince the two gunmen that the legs protruding from beneath the van belonged to a mechanic, because they moved on. They passed from Hutch's view to the pump area in front of the service station.

Looking back at Starsky, Hutch saw that his head was turned in the direction of the front of the station. When he stopped pounding, but remained there, Hutch realized the van was still in the view of the two gunmen, even though he couldn't see them.

Rising to his feet, Hutch put away his gun. When the girl looked at him inquiringly, he said in a low voice, "We wait."

Out front Buckman and Thorn saw Frank Deeks come from the office of the motel across the road. Buckman yelled across to him, "Anything?"

"Not a sign," Deeks yelled back.

They waited for him to cross the road and join them. With their backs to him, Starsky could have made it into the cab of the van, except that Deeks was now facing his way. He stayed where he was.

When Deeks reached this side of the road, he asked Buckman, "You turn anything?"

The heavyset man shook his head. "I got a feeling something's not just right, though."

"Like what?" Deeks asked.

"That guy who runs this place, he seemed a little too definite when we asked if he seen a Checker cab. It either had to pass through here or stop here. Nowhere else it could go."

"The dude in the restaurant too," Thorn said. "He was pretty nervous. The people eating in there was awful quiet, too."

"Maybe they was dead," Buckman said. "Did you see that meat loaf in the pan?"

"Well, they obviously ain't here," Deeks said. "Maybe they got through town without nobody noticing them. You pay for the gas?"

"No," Buckman said. He walked back to glance into the office, saw it was empty, and went over to the corner of the building nearest the restaurant. Looking toward the rear, he called, "Hey, old man!"

When there was no answer, he glanced around in all directions, then remembered Starsky's legs. When Starsky saw him approaching, he picked up the rock again and began pounding on the muffler. Buckman stopped in front of him and kicked the sole of his left foot.

"Hey, you!"

Starsky stopped pounding with the rock, but his heart started pounding in the same tempo. "What yer want?" he inquired in a pronounced Arkansas drawl.

"Where's the old man?"

"Now, how should I know thet, mister?"

He resumed pounding. Buckman kicked his foot again.

Stopping his pounding again, Starsky asked in his Arkansas drawl, "What now?"

"I owe him for some gas. Come on out of there and take the money."

"See Jenson over at the station."

"He's not there."

Buckman started to lean down to peer beneath the van. Raising his right foot, Starsky waggled it near his face.

"Don't tell me yo' troubles," he drawled. "I don't even work heah."

Straightening, Buckman regarded the legs protruding from beneath the van with annoyance, then turned and walked back in front of the service station.

"Why don't we just take off without paying?" Willie Thorn suggested.

Frank Deeks said, "When you been in this business long as we have, kid, you'll learn stuff like that is dumb. You call attention to yourself, maybe get reported to a sheriff, just for a lousy couple of bucks. Let's look around back."

"You look around back," the wounded man said sullenly. "I've done all the walking I'm gonna on this leg."

He went over to the Ford and climbed in the back seat, which put him out of view of the van. Deeks and Buckman started back between the garage and the restaurant toward the rear of the garage.

Starsky hollered, "Hey, Jenson! Couple fellers out here lookin' for yuh! Yuh out back somewheres?"

Behind the garage Hutch got the message. Grabbing
the girl's hand, he dragged her to the back door and
inside. He had barely pulled the door closed when the
two gunmen rounded the corner.

Starsky slid from beneath the van, climbed to his
feet and cautiously peered around the back of the van.
Buckman and Deeks had paused by the back door
into the garage and Deeks was turning the knob.
Starsky's heart leapt into his throat, but then he realized he needn't worry. Obviously Hutch had thrown
the inside bolt, because the pair moved on.

As soon as the two gunmen had rounded the far
corner, Starsky ran to the garage door and gave the
code knock for all clear. He heard the bolt being
drawn, then Hutch and the girl stepped out.

"Let's move it!" Starsky said. "Let's see if we can
get out of here before they complete the circle."

The three ran for the van. Hutch and the girl
climbed in back and Hutch pulled the door closed
from inside. Starsky climbed in through the right-hand
door of the cab, and stepped on a farmer's floppy
straw hat lying on the floor as he slid over under the
wheel.

Pulling off his Rams warm-up cap, he lifted the
straw hat from the floor and jammed it onto his head.
Then he reached up under the dashboard, found the
two ignition wires, twisted them together and hit the
starter. It only groaned.

Groaning also, Starsky hit it again. On the third try
the engine caught. After a couple of sputters, it settled down to run noisily but steadily.

The van had a stick shift. Starsky shifted into low
and eased up on the clutch. The van started off with
a series of jerks because its worn clutch was slipping.
Starsky quickly shifted into second and fed it more
gas.

Buckman and Deeks had completed their circui
of the building when the van started toward the road
They couldn't see the face of the driver, because
floppy straw hat concealed it. They stood watching a

the van turned right when it reached the road, and chugged away toward the south.

From the back Hutch asked, "They buy it?"

With his eyes on the rearview mirror, Starsky said, "So far."

He had shifted into high, but now he shifted back down into second in order to climb the steep grade south of town.

Back at Jenson's Corners Deeks said impatiently, "Let's just leave the damn money on his desk. The amount's registered right there on the pump."

Buckman looked at the pump. It showed 8.3 gallons for $5.24. He dug a five-dollar bill and some change from his pocket and examined the change. He had a quarter, three dimes and a nickel.

"Got four cents?" he asked Deeks.

"Jesus, be big-hearted and leave a penny tip," Deeks told him.

The heavyset man went into the office and laid the five and a quarter in the center of the desk. As he was turning to leave, he noticed the door from the office into the repair garage. Deciding to make one last attempt to find the proprietor, he opened the door and looked in. After staring inside for a moment, he ran to the front door of the office.

"Hey, Deeks!" he called urgently. "Get in here! The cab's in the garage. They pulled a switch!"

Deeks ran into the office and looked into the garage. "Damn!" he said. "Pulled a switch with what?"

"The van!" Buckman said with sudden enlightenment. "He gave them the van!"

He ran outdoors with Deeks racing after him. As he jumped behind the wheel of the Ford, Deeks slid in on the other side.

The engine started, and the Ford took off with a squeal of tortured tires.

Chapter XV

WHEN THE VAN got over the top of the grade, the road again became hilly and winding. Steep drop-offs made it dangerous to drive very fast, but the van couldn't go very fast anyway. Starsky constantly had to shift down on both upgrades and downgrades, and sometimes had to go into low. Once he got used to the slipping clutch, he made the transitions smoothly.

"I'd hate to drive this road at night," Starsky said over his shoulder.

"It's only seven," Hutch said. "You have a good two hours of daylight."

"We'll be on 101 long before that," Joanne said. "The cutoff leading to it is only about ten miles ahead."

About three miles beyond Jenson's Corners they came to a fairly straight section of road running for about a half-mile, all uphill. Just before they rounded a curve at the crest, Starsky glanced into the rearview mirror and caught a glimpse of the yellow Ford at the bottom of the grade.

"They're behind us!" he said.

Drawing his gun, Hutch moved to the back of the van to peer out the rear window. "I don't see them."

"Of course not," Starsky said irritably. "They were a half-mile back. I caught them in the rearview mirror just before we came around that last curve. They're not a half-mile back now, though. They were coming like a bat out of hell."

Hutch said, "We can't outrun them, can we?"

"No way. Got any ideas?"

"No. You?"

Starsky made no immediate reply. They were just starting up another grade steep enough to require shifting into second gear. There was a cliff to their left, and a sheer fifty-foot drop-off to their right, with no guardrail. Ahead the road disappeared around a bend to the left. A sign fifty yards before the bend warned: HAIRPIN CURVE.

After a thorough study of the situation, Starsky finally said, "I'm working on it."

In the rearview mirror he saw the yellow Ford round the curve at the bottom of the grade, no more than two hundred yards behind them. "Make sure that's the same Ford," he said in a strangely calm voice that made Hutch's hair rise slightly. When he used that voice, Starsky was getting ready to do something unorthodox and, as often as not, something suicidally dangerous.

Peering out the back window, Hutch said, "It is. I can recognize Buckman behind the wheel and Deeks sitting next to him."

"Hold on, then," Starsky said.

Even though it was in second gear, the van was traveling at close to forty miles an hour. Starsky negotiated the curve without slowing by moving into the left lane, risking head-on collision if anything was coming the other way around the blind curve. It was the only way he could have made it without slowing, because even then the van's right wheels went off onto the soft shoulder in the middle of the curve, coming within inches of the drop-off.

Both Hutch and the girl closed their eyes and prayed.

Fighting the wheel to get the van back on the road, Starsky managed to whip the heavy vehicle around the curve without going over the edge. The instant he was completely around it, he cramped the front wheels to the left to drive straight at the side of the cliff, and hit the brakes hard. With the front wheels off in the soft dirt of the shoulder, but the rear ones still on the blacktop, the van slewed around 180 degrees to face the other way. Shifting into low, Starsky gunned back the way they had come for a few yards, threw it into second and floored the accelerator.

The yellow Ford rounded the curve at a safely moderate speed. The driver's face became startled at the sight of the van coming at him. Before he could react, the van was roaring past with only a quarter inch between it and the Ford. When nearly past, Starsky cramped the wheel to the right and hit the brakes. The effect was to swing the rear of the van into the left rear fender of the Ford, much as a dirty basketball player might swing his hip against that of an opponent to put him out of the game.

The Ford was sent into a violent, uncontrollable spin. Starsky took his foot off the brake, straightened the wheels and slammed into low gear. The van rocked back and forth a few times, but he finally managed to bring it to a halt on the shoulder.

He watched through the side window and Hutch and the girl watched through the back one as the Ford slid over the edge of the embankment and tumbled end over end down the steep slope. It landed on rocks fifty feet below with a tremendous crash followed by an explosion and a burst of flame.

Hutch expelled a long-held breath. "When you do get an idea, it's a dilly," he said with a touch of awe.

The girl said in a faint voice, "I think I'm going to be sick."

Hutch immediately opened the back door and helped her out. She walked back up the road a few yards, staying on the shoulder and avoiding looking toward the flaming pyre.

Starsky slid across the seat to get out by the right-hand door, and rounded the van to look at its left rear fender. There was a fresh dent in it, but it was hardly noticeable among the old dents.

Hutch had crossed the road to gaze down at the burning Ford. Starsky joined him and they watched the fire together for a time. Finally they both looked in the direction Joanne had walked, and saw her coming back. They recrossed the road to meet her.

"Feel all right now?" Starsky asked.

"I wasn't sick," she said quickly. "I guess I just needed air." She still avoided looking in the direction of the fire.

They all climbed back in the van, and Starsky drove on. Joanne said, "It wasn't just those men dying that got to me. I felt sorry for them, but after all, they were trying to kill us. What nearly made me faint was that stunt. I thought we were going over too."

"Starsky sometimes drives a car like a halfback making a broken field run," Hutch said. "But for ordinary driving he's pretty careful. You can relax now."

They had reached the bottom of the grade where Starsky had first sighted the Ford in the rearview mirror. Hutch said, "When you going to turn around, Starsk? Los Angeles is the other way, you know."

"We're only about three miles from Jenson's Corners," Starsky said. "I figured we might as well go back and get the taxicab."

At the service station Starsky swung past the pumps in order to activate the signal bell inside, swung toward the road again, then backed the van in between the station and the restaurant to park it where it had been before. Unwinding the ignition wires and leaving the straw hat on the floor where he had found it, he put his Rams cap back on and got out of the right side of the cab. Hutch and the girl got out of the back. Together they walked over to meet Abel Jenson as he came from the office.

"We came to pick up the taxi," Starsky said.

"Okay," the filling-station owner said agreeably. He went back into the office and on into the garage.

Hutch said, "I better phone the highway patrol about that car we saw go over the bank," and went into the office also.

A moment later the wide garage door rumbled upward by electric power. Jenson came outdoors again.

"We put a slight dent in the van's left rear fender," Starsky told him.

He led the man over to point it out. While they were looking at it, Hutch joined them. Starsky gave him an inquiring look.

"I didn't give my name," Hutch said. "I explained I just saw it happen, and had no information other than the location. The sergeant I talked to understood."

Jenson said, "New fender costs about a hundred bucks."

"If you put one on," Starsky agreed. "But since you haven't replaced it for any of those previous dents, I doubt that you will do it for this one. You wouldn't even have noticed it if I hadn't pointed it out."

"Maybe I wouldn't put a new one on," Jenson said. "But the guy who owns it might want one. And I'm not about to pay for it."

"All right," Starsky gave in. "We'll say a hundred."

Jenson's eyes brightened and he held out his hand expectantly. Starsky held out his, too.

"So just return a hundred of the two I gave you and we'll be even," Starsky said.

"Return a hundred!" Jenson said indignantly.

With his hand still outthrust, palm up, Starsky said, "If you think you're getting two hundred bucks for a half-hour rental on that bucket of bolts, you've got rocks in your head. Two hundred was for driving it to Los Angeles, and all the trouble of getting it back to you. We only drove it around the block. Now get it up, or I'll place you under arrest for price-gouging."

The man tried to stare Starsky down, but averted his gaze rather quickly. Reluctantly he took out a roll of bills and separated two of the fifties Starsky had given him.

Pocketing them, Starsky asked, "What *do* you consider a fair rental for a half hour?"

"Five bucks, maybe?" Jenson said hopefully.

"Seems fair," Starsky said, holding out his hand again. "So I'll take back five of that ten I gave you for gas. We couldn't have used more than two bits worth."

"Hey, that's not fair," the service-station proprietor protested.

"I could also review the thirty-dollar charge you made for storing the cab," Starsky said. "But I don't want to be unreasonable. You did us a thirty-dollar favor."

"Well, I should hope so," Jenson said aggrievedly. "Them fellows looked dangerous. I took some risk, lying to them that I hadn't seen you."

"Thirty dollars' worth of risk," Starsky agreed. "Not thirty-five. So come up with the five."

Again reluctantly, Jenson handed over a five.

"Cheer up," Starsky said as he pocketed it. "A hundred and thirty profit in about an hour and a half isn't bad for a dump like this."

As he and Hutch walked back to rejoin the girl, Hutch said, "You're kind of a scrooge, aren't you?"

"Because I don't like to get cheated?" Starsky asked. "He still got overpaid. I know it's department money, not out of my own pocket, but it's the principle of the thing."

The three of them walked into the garage together and climbed into the cab, Hutch and the girl again getting into the back seat and Starsky driving.

"Watch this," Starsky said. "He won't be mad at me. He still figures he took us for suckers."

As they pulled out of the garage, Starsky threw the filling-station proprietor a friendly wave. He got one back just as friendly.

When they passed the place where the Ford had gone over the bank, the fire was out, and two highway patrol cars were parked on the shoulder. They didn't stop.

About ten miles beyond Jenson's Corners they came to the first crossroad they had seen in over a hundred miles. A sign with an arrow pointing to the right said: TO HIGHWAY 101: LOS ANGELES–SAN FRANCISCO.

By now it was nearing 8 P.M. As they turned right,

the girl said, "I'm getting awfully hungry. There's a
good restaurant called the Golden Squirrel on this road
about fifteen miles from here, just before you hit the
freeway."

"I could stand some dinner too," Hutch said.

"I guess I could eat some dessert," Starsky said.
"I already had dinner."

"Don't spoil my appetite by talking about that,"
Hutch requested.

Chapter XVI

THE GOLDEN SQUIRREL was a dinner house with a
cocktail lounge to the left and a dining room to the
right of a spacious lobby. A hostess showed them to
a table in the dining room. When their waitress came,
they ordered cocktails while they looked over the
menus. Hutch had a martini, Joanne a manhattan, and
Starsky a beer.

By the time the waitress brought the drinks, they
had all decided what they wanted to eat. Hutch and the
girl ordered prime rib, Starsky a piece of cherry pie
à la mode.

When the waitress moved away, Hutch raised his
cocktail glass and said, "To survival."

They all sipped. When they set down their glasses,
Joanne said, "We came close to not surviving." Then
she had a sudden thought. "My father will be worried
sick. He expected me hours ago. I should phone the
hospital."

Starsky and Hutch looked at each other. Hutch said,
"You're having the same thought I am, huh?"

"Uh-huh. Joanne, there's two cops in your father's room, and we don't know who the leak is."

After considering this, she said, "Couldn't we at least get word to him that I'm safe?"

Hutch said, "We might do that, if we can figure out somebody to phone that we can trust."

"We could phone Dobey," Starsky suggested.

In a harsh voice Hutch said, "Aside from us, only Dobey and Coleman knew we were coming after Joanne. Look at that fact from all angles and see what you come up with."

Starsky thought this over thoroughly. Eventually he said, "I can't see Dobey as the leak."

"I hate to think he'd be," Hutch said. "But Coleman can't be. If he was on Kester's side, he just wouldn't push getting him indicted. You know a D.A. has almost total discretion in what indictments he asks for. Coleman dug up that old Morgan case to pressure Joanne's father into testifying. It just doesn't make sense that he'd go to all this trouble to stop him."

"What's the old Morgan case?" the girl asked.

"Oh, just something that happened a long time ago," Hutch said vaguely.

Starsky was pensively sipping his beer. Then he sat up straight as a thought struck him. "I just solved it," he said. "Can you really see the captain as the leak?"

"Not really," Hutch admitted. "I just can't think of any other answer."

"I just did. His office is bugged."

Hutch stared at him. "Of course," he said in a wondering voice. "Why didn't that occur to anybody before?" Glancing at his watch, he got up from his chair. "Just eight-thirty. He ought to be at home. I saw a pay phone in the lobby on the way in. I'm going to give him a ring."

He took change from his pocket and looked at it. "Forty-five cents. You got any change?"

Starsky produced eighty cents.

"That ought to do it," Hutch said. He moved off toward the lobby.

In the phone booth he direct-dialed the captain's home number, then an operator came on and asked him for sixty-five cents more. The phone began to ring on the other end, and Captain Dobey's voice said, "Hello."

"Hutch, Captain. Just phoned to tell you we're all right. Will you call the hospital to let Mello know his daughter is okay?"

"Hutch, where the hell are you?" Dobey asked. "I got an APB out on you people."

"You can cancel it, Captain. We're all fine. We decided to drive back instead of fly, is all, after some characters tried to squeeze us on the way to the airport."

"One of them Sid Johnson?"

"Kester's second-in-command?" Hutch said in surprise. "Could have been. Why?"

"We got word he was found shot to death in a stolen car just outside Bryland. I figured that related to you guys not showing up."

"It did, but we didn't know it was Johnson. You'll get word about three other Kester goons burning up in another car, if they're identifiable."

"Who's that?"

"Frank Deeks, Buck Buckman, and Willie Thorn."

After some silence, the captain said, "No great loss to society. Want to tell me about it?"

"It can wait. We'll put it in our report."

"All right," Dobey consented. "Where are you now?"

"That's unimportant, Captain. Just tell Mello we'll have his daughter at the hospital tomorrow morning."

"What do you mean, it's unimportant? Where the hell are you?"

Hutch said patiently, "Captain, Harry Kester knew we were picking up Joanne Mello. Think about who could have told him. Who knew besides me and Starsk?"

There was a long wait before Captain Dobey said, "Coleman and me."

"Right. And Coleman wouldn't have a reason in the world to tip Kester. If he was in Kester's pocket, he simply wouldn't ask the grand jury to indict him."

"Are you accusing me of being the leak?" Captain Dobey asked ominously.

"No. Starsky figured out what the leak was just a couple of minutes ago."

"What? You mean who."

"No, I mean what. There's a bug in your office."

This time the silence went on so long that Hutch asked, "Did you hear me?"

"Yes," Dobey said in a tone of self-disgust. "Why the hell didn't I think of that?"

"There may be one on your phone too, Captain. Which is why I don't care to tell you where we are."

"I understand, Hutch," the captain said in a considerably mellower voice. "See you in the morning."

Hutch hung up, started to leave the booth, then stopped and picked up the receiver again when the phone rang.

"Please deposit forty-five cents for overtime," the crisp voice of the operator said.

Hutch deposited the money and hung up. When he got back to the table, his and Joanne's salads and Starsky's pie à la mode had been delivered. As he sat down, both Starsky and the girl gave him inquiring looks.

"He'll phone the hospital," Hutch said. "I told him his office was bugged, and he wondered why he hadn't thought of that."

He finished his cocktail and dug into his salad. From the corner of his eye he saw Starsky take a sip of beer, eat a bit of cherry pie and ice cream, and chase it with another sip of beer.

Setting down his fork, Hutch said, "Starsk, how can you mix beer and cherry pie à la mode?"

"I'm not mixing them," Starsky said, looking up at him. "I'm alternating."

By the time the prime-rib dinners were delivered, Starsky had finished both his dessert and his beer. He ordered a cup of coffee to sip on while he watched the other two eat.

As he cut into his prime rib, Hutch asked, "Where are we going to stash Joanne tonight after we get to L.A.?"

"She'd be safe at my place," Starsky said.

"Or mine."

Joanne looked from one to the other. "Neither of your wives would mind?"

"We don't have any," Starsky said.

"Oh. How many beds at your place?"

"One."

She looked at Hutch.

"One," he admitted.

"Got any other suggestions?" she asked dryly.

Starsky and Hutch looked at each other.

"Why don't we just grab a motel with connecting rooms somewhere between here and Los Angeles?" Starsky suggested. "Nobody will know where we are, and in the remote event anybody nasty does drop in, we'll be right next door to foil them."

That's what they decided to do.

They rented motel rooms in Thousand Oaks, only forty-five minutes from downtown Los Angeles. In the morning they were on the road again by six, which got them to Los Angeles too early to call at the hospital. They drove by Starsky's place, where Starsky changed clothes, loaned Hutch a change of underwear and socks and a clean shirt, and both shaved.

They got to the hospital at 8 A.M.. The two uniformed men posted in the hall at the end of the dead-end corridor on the fifth floor recognized the detectives and passed them into the hospital room. The two policemen inside knew them also. When Starsky gestured toward the door and said, "Take a break," they nodded and left.

A pretty woman in her mid-twenties was just taking a breakfast tray from Andrew Mello. When they first entered the room, both Starsky and Hutch had assumed she was a nurse, but now they saw it wasn't a white uniform she was wearing, merely a white dress. She was about the same height and build as the girl they had brought into the room, also had dark hair and much the same coloring, although their features weren't very similar.

"Everything go all right?" the girl with Starsky and Hutch asked.

The one in the white dress smiled and nodded. "No problems. How about you?"

"We had a few moments."

Indicating the patient, the girl in the white dress said, "This is my father, Andrew Mello, Linda. Linda Williams, Father."

Mello cordially held out his hand, and the girl clasped it in greeting.

"I appreciate what you've done," the ex-racketeer said sincerely.

Starsky and Hutch looked at each other in bewilderment. Hutch inquired loudly, "Would somebody mind telling us what the hell's going on here?"

Turning to them, the girl they had been calling Joanne Mello all along indicated the other girl and said, "Starsky, Hutch, this is Joanne Mello. My name is Detective Linda Williams, San Francisco Police."

Producing an ID, she showed it to the two stunned detectives.

Chapter XVII

STARSKY AND HUTCH looked at each other. Starsky said in a tone of outrage, "We were decoys! And they didn't even let us in on it!"

Hutch growled at the woman detective. "You put on a hell of a good act, Detective Williams. All that crap about how great your father was under his rotten exterior, and how concerned you were for his welfare. You almost had us crying."

"I was just following instructions," she said defensively. "I was told to make it convincing."

"You deserve an Oscar," Starsky said sourly.

"You don't have to take it out on me," the girl said with a touch of spirit. "I'm a cop just like you, and I follow instructions. Don't you two follow instructions?"

"Not when they're stupid," Hutch told her.

"What did I know about you two?" she flared at him. "It was made very definite to me that you were not to suspect I wasn't the real Joanne Mello. Don't blame me for not trusting you. It was your own department that didn't trust you."

Starsky and Hutch looked at each other again. "She's right," Hutch said. "We're getting mad at the wrong person. We should be mad at our lovable and trusting captain."

"I'm mad at everybody," Starsky said.

Hutch turned to the real Joanne Mello. "What are security arrangements for you, Miss Mello? Where are you staying?"

"Right here last night, in the room next door. With a policewoman guard."

"You'll be going with your father when he's released from here and we move him to a safe house?"

Mello said, "She's going somewhere safer than that. I'm sending her out of the country."

"Oh?" Hutch said. "Where?"

"Paris. I have an associate there who will assure her safety until this thing is over. His status in Paris is about what mine was in Los Angeles before I took my fall. Nobody will be about to touch her over there, so long as she's under my friend's protection."

"When?" Hutch asked.

"That's up to Captain Dobey. He's handling all arrangements, including whatever security measures are necessary to get Joanne from here to the airport."

Hutch turned to Starsky. "Let's get over to Dobey's office."

Both detectives strode from the room. Linda Williams hurried after them, catching them at the elevator. Starsky savagely pushed the call button. They waited silently for the door to open, and also rode the elevator down without a word. In the parking lot neither offered to hold the cab door open for the woman detective. Starsky slid behind the steering wheel. Hutch got in front next to his partner. Linda opened the rear door herself and climbed in back.

As they pulled off the lot, the girl said, "I thought you decided you were mad at your division head, not me."

"I clearly announced I was mad at everybody," Starsky said shortly.

Hutch said, "I'm not mad at you. I just don't feel very friendly. I don't like to be played for a sucker."

Linda sighed. "All right. I'll be out of your hair soon. Meantime, does my punishment include starvation?"

Hutch turned sidewise in the seat to look around at her. "What's that mean?"

"It's nearly eight-thirty, and we haven't had any breakfast."

"We have," Starsky said with a touch of sadistic satisfaction. "Didn't you see the sign in your room that the motel served free continental breakfast in the lobby from five-thirty on? Hutch and I had rolls and coffee."

"Well, thanks a bunch for inviting me," she said indignantly.

"The sign was your invitation," Starsky said. "It's not our fault that San Francisco cops can't read."

"You know what, Starsky?" she said. "I'm beginning to get just as mad as you are."

"He's only trying to get your goat," Hutch soothed her. "There's a cafeteria at Parker Center where you can get some breakfast. Actually we were just trying to be kind by letting you sleep longer."

When they reached Parker Center, Starsky drove the Checker cab into the underground garage. When he parked it in front of the dispatcher's office and they all got out, the dispatcher came out of his office.

"What's this? he asked. "You can't park that thing down here, Starsky."

"It's going in the repair shop," Starsky said. "We're in kind of a hurry, Hal, so will you make out the work order for me? Needs a side and a rear window, those shotgun pellet dents filled and sanded, the bullet holes plugged, and a new paint job."

"You can't have a privately owned vehicle repaired at public expense," the dispatcher protested.

"You can when it's been commandeered by the police and damaged during use on official police business," Starsky told him. "The owner will be coming from San Francisco to pick it up. His ID's on the back of the front seat. If the mechanics do a good job, we may not get sued."

"Oh," the dispatcher said. "In that case you can leave it there. Your car is all ready, incidentally, and is parked in its usual slot."

"Fine," Starsky said. He moved on to rejoin Hutch

and Linda, who were already waiting at the elevator.

As they stepped into the elevator car, Hutch pushed the button for the third floor. When the car started up, he said, "Cafeteria's on the eighth floor, Detective Williams. When you've had breakfast, you can come down to Captain Dobey's office on third."

Looking from one to the other, she said, "You're not coming with me?"

"We're a little eager to see our revered leader," Starsky said dryly.

Sighing again, she said, "Boy, you guys sure hold a grudge. But okay. I guess it won't hurt me to skip breakfast. I've been planning to start a diet anyway, and keep putting it off."

They found District Attorney Don Coleman with the captain in Dobey's office. Both courteously rose to their feet at sight of the girl.

When neither Starsky nor Hutch showed any inclination to introduce her, Linda said to the man behind the desk, "Captain Dobey?"

"Yes?"

"I'm Detective Linda Williams of the San Francisco Police."

"Glad to know you, Detective Williams," the captain said cordially. He indicated the D.A. "This is District Attorney Donald Coleman."

Coleman smiled and nodded at the girl and she asked him how he did. Captain Dobey invited her to have a seat. Starsky and Hutch stood there looking irked by all these formalities.

The girl sat against the wall next to Coleman. Dobey resumed his seat and looked at Starsky and Hutch.

"Find the bug?" Starsky asked conversationally.

The captain shook his head. "There wasn't any. Within fifteen minutes of my conversation with Hutch, I had experts going over this office with a fine-tooth comb. It isn't bugged. Neither is Coleman's, and neither of our phones are tapped."

Coleman said, "Which means the leak is a person. A person in this division."

Starsky and Hutch both glanced at him, then returned their attention to Dobey. Hutch said sardonically, "We appreciate your faith in us, Captain."

Starsky, whose quiet manner so far had been masking a smoldering anger, erupted. "A setup!" he spat at Dobey. "You set us up!"

"Now wait a minute, Starsky—" the captain started to say.

"You needed a decoy?" Starsky said. "Okay! Someone to attract Kester's attention while the San Francisco police bring Mello's daughter down here? Okay! A little kinky, but workable." He carefully pronounced each of the words in his next sentence. "But—why—weren't—we—in—on—it?"

"I wanted to tell you," Dobey growled. "I couldn't."

"What do you mean, you couldn't?"

"I wouldn't let him," Coleman said.

Starsky and Hutch both turned to stare at the district attorney. Hutch said, "*You* wouldn't let him? Who the hell's running this division?"

"I'm running it," Captain Dobey said in a definite tone. "But this was the D.A.'s show, and I had to go along."

In a quiet but firm voice Coleman said, "Listen, you two. Mello said Kester had somebody in his pocket. You guessed it was a bug, and we proved that wrong. What happened proved Mello was right. When a division is suspect, everyone in that division is suspect. Dobey said he trusted you two. I told him that with what was at stake, I couldn't afford to trust anybody."

Stunned, the two detectives considered this. Starsky slumped into a chair on the opposite side of the room from the district attorney and the woman detective.

"Terrific," Starsky said.

Hutch said to Linda, "Did you know we were suspected of being the leak?"

"I had been informed there was a leak," she said.

"When I was also told to make sure you never caught on that I wasn't Joanne Mello, I had to assume you were under suspicion."

"Oh, great," Hutch said. "Didn't it occur to you that if we were working for Kester, we would have turned you over to those goons instead of risking our necks to keep them away from you?"

"Get off her back," Coleman suggested dourly. "She risked her neck too. And I, for one, am very grateful."

After staring at the man for a moment, Hutch said sardonically, "My apologies, Detective Williams. The next time we're set up for a wipeout, I hope you'll join us again." He turned to Starsky. "Come on, Starsk. Let's get out of here."

Starsky got up and the pair headed for the door.

"Where do you think you're going?" Dobey inquired. "We're not through with you yet."

The two detectives stopped and turned. "What next?" Starsky asked. "You gonna shoot us out of a cannon?"

"Come back and sit down," Dobey ordered.

There was no noticeable change in the big black man's tone detectable to Coleman and the girl, but Starsky and Hutch had worked under the captain long enough to recognize certain nuances. They could tell that he had taken all the guff he intended to from his subordinates, and a push of even another fraction of an inch would bring an explosion. Starsky returned to his chair, and Hutch sat beside him. Their expressions were hardly subservient, but they ceased being belligerent.

Having put them in their places, the captain temporarily ignored them to turn his attention to the girl. He said, "Andrew Mello wants his daughter out of the country, Detective Williams."

"Yes, I know. He told us that at the hospital."

"Oh, you've been to the hospital?"

She nodded. "Just before we came here."

"Did he tell you where he's sending her?"

She nodded again. "To Paris, under the protection

of some friend of his whom I gathered was a Parisian racketeer."

"The biggest one, apparently," Dobey said. "The plane leaves from International Airport at four o'clock this afternoon. How would you like to accompany her?"

"I think I could handle that," Linda said, her face lighting up. "Providing my superiors authorize it."

Coleman said, "I already cleared it with San Francisco. That doesn't commit you, of course. I merely got conditional clearance, in the event you accepted the assignment. Captain Dobey can appoint a local policewoman if you don't want it."

"I would love it," she assured him.

"In that case you have it," Dobey said. Switching on his intercom, he said "Terry, make that voucher for the Paris trip to Detective Linda Williams, on special duty to the L.A.P.D. from the San Francisco Police. And bring it in for her signature as soon as it's typed up."

"Yes, sir," Terry Evers' voice said from the speaker.

Glancing at his watch, Coleman got to his feet. "I have to get to my office." He moved to the door, turned back to say, "Nice to have met you, Detective Williams. Good luck on your trip to Paris."

"The kiss of death," Starsky muttered inaudibly.

The D.A. must have had acute hearing, because he gave him a sharp glance. But he left without saying anything.

Chapter XVIII

CAPTAIN DOBEY TURNED to his two detectives. "While we're waiting for Terry, tell me just what happened up there?"

Hutch said, "Four guns in two cars tried to squeeze us just outside Bryland. Starsky gunned one, who I guess turned out to be Sid Johnson, although we didn't know that at the time. I nicked Willie Thorn in the leg. We made a run for it, and the surviving three chased us in one car. They caught up with us on a mountain road about a hundred and sixty miles south of Bryland, near a place called Jenson's Corners. Starsky was driving, and he nudged them off the road. They crashed and burned. That's about it."

"You'll have to stick it in a written report," the captain said. "And in considerably more detail. What about the taxicab?"

"How'd you know about it?"

"Guy named George Shetland phoned the chief from San Francisco, said you commandeered his cab and left him a watch for security. A quite expensive one, he said. I assume that was the fancy watch you showed me, Starsky."

Starsky nodded. "But I didn't leave it. Hutch did." He threw his partner an aggrieved look.

"Shetland claimed the cab was pretty shot up," Dobey said. "Demanded full repairs, a paint job, plane fare from San Francisco to pick it up, and five hundred dollars compensation for his time and trouble."

"Give it to him," Hutch advised. "He earned every penny of it. He might get five thousand if he sued."

Starsky said, "The repairs and paint job are already being taken care of."

Terry Evers came in, carrying the familiar clipboard and three envelopes. "Detective Williams?" she said to Linda.

"Yes."

The secretary handed her the three envelopes. "Two plane tickets to Paris and cash for expenses. Sign here, please."

She handed over the clipboard and a pen, and pointed to where she wanted Linda to sign.

Captain Dobey said, "Hutch, you and Starsky are going to deliver Detective Williams and Joanne Mello to the airport. Her reservation's under the name Sandra Small, incidentally."

Terry threw a startled side-glance at the captain.

"Better get to the hospital to pick up Miss Mello by two at least," Dobey continued. "I'll meet you there, because I want to talk to Miss Mello before she leaves."

"All right," Hutch agreed. He rose to his feet. "That all?"

"For now."

Starsky also got up. The secretary recovered her clipboard and pen and left the room.

Starsky said, "I guess we got time to buy you that breakfast you missed now, Linda."

The girl looked at him in surprise. "It's not Detective Williams anymore? I thought you were mad at everybody."

"Nobody stays mad forever," Starsky said. "Wanna kiss and make up?"

"I'm willing to make up," she said, getting to her feet. "But it looks silly for a couple of cops to kiss each other."

In the outer office, Terry Evers waited a couple of minutes after the two male detectives and the woman detective departed, then went up the corridor to a pay phone. She dropped in a dime, dialed a number, and when a feminine voice said, "Kester Enterprises," she said, "Mr. Kester, please. This is Terry."

"Just a moment, please."

It was several moments before the racketeer's voice said, "Yes, Terry?"

The secretary said rapidly, "Starsky and Hutch rolled in with a woman Joanne Mello's age and description a while ago. At first I thought she was the Mello girl, but I listened at the captain's door long enough to realize she was a policewoman from San Francisco. Your men messed up. That's who they were chasing, not Mello's daughter."

"Jesus," Kester said. "It was on the air that Sid Johnson cashed in. Over a decoy! What happened to the other three, I don't know. I haven't heard from them."

"You won't," she said. "They cashed in too."

"That goddamned Starsky and Hutch!" Kester flared. "Those were good men."

"Mello's daughter's at the hospital with her dad," Terry said. "Presumably under tight security. Starsky and Hutch and this woman cop from San Francisco are going to pick her up at two P.M. to take her to the airport. She's flying to Paris at four under the name Sandra Small."

"Paris?" Kester said. "Jesus, he must be sending her under the protection of his buddy René DuBois. If she ever gets there, she's beyond our reach. You sure about this?"

"Of course I'm sure. I booked the flight."

"Maybe you ought to cancel the reservations," Kester growled.

The secretary giggled. "Maybe I should. The airlines hate no-shows."

In the eighth-floor cafeteria Linda chose a sweet roll and a cup of coffee. Since it had now been three and a half hours since their scanty breakfast, both Starsky and Hutch decided to have something too. Hutch chose a container of yogurt and a glass of buttermilk. Starsky asked one of the girls behind the counter if she could make him a special sandwich.

"Sure," she said. "If we've got the ingredients."

Hutch and Linda moved on to get a table, leaving Starsky to wait for his sandwich. They were seated side by side at one of the long tables when Starsky approached and sat across from them. In addition to his sandwich, he had a glass of some dark-colored drink.

"What is that?" Hutch asked as Starsky took a bite from his sandwich.

"Dr. Pepper."

"I mean the sandwich. Dr. Pepper! Whoever heard of Dr. Pepper for breakfast?"

"They were out of root beer. It's peanut butter and bacon."

Hutch gave him a pained look. "Starsky, I swear you dream up these combinations just to turn my stomach."

Starsky chewed with enjoyment and swallowed before saying, "What you think your health food does to mine? What's that glop?"

"Banana yogurt."

Making a face, Starsky said to the girl, "See? He criticizes my palate, then eats glue like that."

"I think I'll stay neutral," she said diplomatically. "I just got back on speaking terms with both of you."

Glancing at his watch, Hutch said, "It's nine A.M. By the time Starsky and I write up our report and finish arguing with Accounting over what we spent on this junket, it may be noon. You don't want to hang around here all morning, do you, Linda? Want us to run you somewhere?"

"I'd like to do a little shopping," the girl said. "I didn't come prepared for Paris. I have a fair amount of clothing in my suitcase, but—" She came to an abrupt halt. "My suitcase! It's in the trunk of that taxicab. My coat too!"

"No problem," Starsky told her. "We'll get them out when we go back downstairs."

When they finished breakfast, they took the elevator

to the basement, got Linda's suitcase and coat from the taxicab and transferred them to the trunk of the Torino. They dropped the girl off at Bullock's Department Store on Broadway, and arranged to pick her up again at the same spot at noon sharp.

Then they returned to Parker Center to do the necessary but most hated part of their job: paperwork. Starsky left Hutch in the squad room to write up the report of what had happened on their trip, while he went to the accounting office to turn in their unused flight tickets and the unspent balance of their expense money, and to explain what they had done with the rest.

As soon as Harry Kester hung up the phone after his conversation with Terry Evers, he switched on his intercom. "Ellie, get Jefko, Tober, and Curly in here," he said. "Is Dippy back in town yet?"

"Yes, sir. He phoned in this morning."

"Get him over here too."

"With his motorbike, Mr. Kester?"

"I don't care what he rides over here, but we won't need that."

"Yes, sir," she said. "I'll take care of it right away."

A few moments later Curly Dobbs, his arm still in a sling, came into the office. A few minutes after that Max Jefko and Jeremy Tober entered. Jefko was a leather-hard man in his forties with unnaturally large wrists and arms. On his left wrist he wore an oversized black-dialed watch. Tober was a knife-thin man in his mid-thirties with a hooked nose and predatory eyes. Curly Dobbs took his usual place at one end of the sofa against the wall. The other two sat in a pair of the leather easy chairs.

Kester opened the meeting by announcing, "I've got some bad news. In addition to Sid Johnson, who you already know about, Buckman, Deeks, and Thorn were all wiped out."

"Creepers," Max Jefko said. "How?"

"I don't know the details yet, except that Starsky and Hutch are responsible."

"It was one of them put the slug in my shoulder," Curly Dobbs growled.

"The worst part is that they were chasing a decoy," Kester said. "A female cop from San Francisco who looks like Joanne Mello. The cops pulled a switch and got the Mello girl down here some other way."

"Creepers," Jefko said. "What a lousy trick."

"Anyway, we've got the Mello girl pinpointed now. She's at Southern Memorial Hospital with her father."

"Want us to go get her?" the leathery Jefko asked.

"Security around the old man is too tight. But I got a tip that Starsky and Hutch and that woman cop from San Francisco will be picking her up at the hospital at two P.M. to take her to the airport. She has a four P.M. reservation on a flight to Paris." He looked at his watch. "It's only nine now, so we've got five hours to figure something out."

"Maybe we could catch them in the parking lot as they're leaving," thin Jeremy Tober suggested.

Kester shook his head. "That's when Starsky and Hutch will be most on guard. Your best bet is to catch them by surprise somewhere they'll least be expecting it."

"What floor's Mello on?" Jefko asked.

"Fifth."

"Then they have to come down on the elevator. We could take them as they get off."

Harry Kester looked dubious. "They're a little sharp to fall for that. An ear I have at the hospital told me that when they took Mello up from the emergency room to the fifth floor, Starsky and Hutch went up alone first, leaving the old man guarded by some other cops. Starsky stayed up there to cover the hallway, while Hutch brought the car back down to get Mello. My guess is they'll do the reverse when they bring Mello's daughter downstairs."

"There's one place they sure as hell won't expect to be hit," Tober said. "On the fifth floor."

Everyone looked at him curiously. Kester said, "Wouldn't that be kind of dangerous?"

"Why? Max and me will need one more guy, just to hold the elevator for us on the fifth floor. We'll catch them just as they get to the elevator, gun down the cops, grab the girl, and drag her on the elevator before the smoke clears."

Everyone considered this. Finally Kester said, "Where you going to pop out from? Starsky and Hutch will sweep that hall clear of any visitors before they start down it with the girl."

Tober said, "I got that figured. We'll be in doctors' uniforms, or attendants' uniforms, or something like that."

Max Jefko's eyes brightened. "That ought to work."

"Okay," Kester said. "One thing, though. I understand this San Francisco policewoman looks pretty much like the Mello girl. How you going to know which is which?"

"Simple," Tober told him. "We'll be watching the parking lot when Starsky and Hutch and the female cop get there. That'll tell us who the cop is, so we grab the other one."

The racket boss nodded approval. "Okay, get on over there and case the layout. Twice Starsky and Hutch have managed to louse us up, and this time I don't want any slips."

"You can count on us, boss," Tober said, getting to his feet. "We'll be thinking about the bonus." He looked at Curly Dobbs. "Think you could run an elevator with that bum wing?"

"Get somebody like Schultz," Kester said. "I've got something else for Curly to do this afternoon."

After the two men had left, Dobbs asked, "What you got for me this afternoon?"

"A chore. Dippy Marrs is on his way over to help you with it."

"With what?" the bald man asked.

"I don't want Max and Jeremy to know I lack complete faith in them, but in case they goof up, I got a backup plan. That bum left arm don't keep you from handling a gun, does it?"

Dobbs shook his head. " 'Course not. I'm right-handed."

"Have Dippy pick up a panel truck somewhere. The two of you be on the airport parking lot from about two-thirty on. If Starsky and Hutch manage to get the Mello girl past Max and Jeremy, you two take her there."

Nodding his bald head, Curly Dobbs said, "Gotcha."

Chapter XIX

IT WAS ABOUT 10 A.M. when Max Jefko, Jeremy Tober, and Arnie Schultz arrived at the hospital. Arnie Schultz was a youngster no more than twenty, tall and angular and badly pimpled. The leathery Jefko, who was driving, parked as near the side door as he could get. The trio got out, glanced around in all directions, and went in by the side door.

The door was at the rear right-hand corner of the building, and opened onto a wide ramp leading down-ward to the emergency room in the basement. On either side of the ramp were short stairways, consisting of only three steps each, leading up to doors giving access to the main floor. They took the right-hand stairs.

The main-floor hall ran straight ahead of them to the opposite side of the building. Halfway along it another hallway running toward the lobby at the front of the building formed a T with it. About fifty feet before the T, on the left side of the hallway, were two

elevators. Just before them was a door lettered
STAIRS.

The three went past doors labeled RADIOLOGY, X-RAY,
SURGERY, and LABORATORY, past the one labeled
STAIRS, to the elevators. The left-hand elevator was
on the main floor. They got on, and the thin Tober
examined the control panel.

"See this button, Arnie?" he asked the pimpled
youth, pointing to one lettered HOLD.

Arnie nodded.

Tober pressed it with his thumb. "Now nobody can
call the car to another floor. Long as you keep the
button pushed in, it stays right where it is with the
door open."

Arnie nodded again.

A nurse and a white-coated doctor came along and
got into the car. Tober quickly took his thumb from
the hold button and pressed 2. He stepped aside and
the nurse pressed 4.

When the three got off on the second floor, a soft
but carrying feminine voice was saying from a speaker
in the hallway, "Dr. Ferris, please. Paging Dr. Ferris."

Tober led the way along the hall in the direction of
the parking lot. From a window at the end of the hall,
directly over the side door, they could get a complete
view of the parking lot.

"We'll post ourselves here about one-thirty," Tober
said. "Any earlier than that, and somebody might
start wondering why we're standing around so long.
But at that time they'll just think we're waiting for
visiting hours to start at two."

"Okay," Jefko said. "So from here we get a good
look at the female detective. Then what?"

"That we figure out next," Tober said. "One thing at
a time."

He led the way back to the elevators. The floor
indicator showed that the left elevator was on the
eighth floor. The other elevator was in the basement.
When Tober pressed the call button, the indicator

panel showed that the car on eight was descending. The *B* on the other panel didn't change.

Pointing to that panel, Tober said, "See, Arnie, some guy's got his finger on the hold button. Probably loading or unloading a patient."

They took the elevator to the fifth floor. The hallways there were laid out identically to those on the first floor. They walked the fifty feet to the intersecting corridor leading to the front of the building. Halfway along it on the left there was a nurses' station. At its far end they could see two uniformed cops sitting in chairs against the wall. After one brief glance that way, the two hit men and the youth stepped back around the corner out of the cops' sight.

"They'll be coming along that hall and around the corner just fifty feet from the elevator," Tober said. "We'll hit 'em just after they turn the corner. Let's see what's this way."

As he led the way past the elevators, the same soft but carrying feminine voice said from a speaker, "Dr. Ferris, please. Paging Dr. Ferris."

Beyond the elevators all but one room on both sides of the hall were hospital rooms. That room, on the opposite side of the hall from the elevators and just beyond them, had LINEN AND SURGICAL SUPPLIES lettered on its door. The door was open, and through it they could see into a large room with shelves all around the walls. A bulky young man of about twenty-five with a moon face and a good deal of fat padding his body stood behind a counter.

"Wait here," Tober said to the other two, and entered the room.

"Yes?" the bulky young man said inquiringly.

"Looking for Dr. Ferris," Tober said.

"He hasn't been here," the attendant said puzzledly. "Ask at the nurses' station around the corner."

"I did," Tober said. "They told me to try surgery."

"That's on first, mister. This is surgical *supplies.*"

"Oh," Tober said. He glanced around the room curiously. The shelves contained sheets and pillowcases, he saw, towels and washcloths, hospital pajamas, doctor's whites, surgical masks, and a variety of other items. There was one row of shelves containing such equipment as bedpans and thermometers, for instance. He said, "You got an awful lot of stuff in here."

"About everything a hospital needs except drugs," the attendant said with a grin. "From bedpans to stethoscopes."

"Must keep you busy," Tober commented. He turned around and walked out.

They took the elevator down to the basement. In the corridor outside the emergency room a half-dozen gurneys were lined up against the wall. Viewing them with satisfaction, Tober said, "I guess that does it. Let's get out of here."

Back out in the parking lot, Tober asked, "What time is it?"

The leathery Jefko looked at his oversized wristwatch. "Ten-thirty."

"Three hours," Tober said. "Arnie, we'll drop you downtown. We'll need a panel truck for the snatch. Hot-wire one and pick up Max and me at my place no later than a quarter of one. Okay?"

Arnie nodded. "I'll be there."

Linda Williams was waiting on the designated corner when Starsky and Hutch got there at noon. She was carrying a small, new-looking suitcase. Starsky pulled the red-and-white Torino over to the curb, cut the ignition, and handed the keys to Hutch. The blond detective jumped out, opened the trunk and took the suitcase from the policewoman. After slamming the trunk shut, he held the door for the girl to get in the back seat, climbed back in front, and returned the keys to Starsky.

As they pulled away, Starsky said, "Bought a new suitcase?"

"I had to. There's no room in my other suitcase for the new clothes I bought."

"It felt full," Hutch said.

"It is. You can't go to Paris without the proper clothing."

"Feel like some lunch?" Starsky asked.

"I guess," she agreed.

Starsky drove to Huggy Bear's and was lucky enough to find a parking place right in front. As usual at that time of day all the booths and tables were filled, but there was room at the bar. When Linda said she didn't mind sitting there, they took three stools at the far end, Starsky around at the side extension of the bar, Linda at the curving corner, and Hutch on the first stool of the main part of the bar.

Huggy Bear was on duty. When he came over, Hutch said, "Huggy Bear, this is Detective Linda Williams of the San Francisco Police. Huggy Bear, Linda, the proprietor of this joint."

"Don't call this joint a joint," Huggy Bear said. "How are you, Linda? I is innocent. I ain't been in San Francisco for years."

"She isn't after you," Starsky said. "Just your food. The word's spread clear to San Francisco, so don't disappoint her."

"No foolin'?" Huggy Bear said, pleased. "You heard about our food clear up there?"

"Smelled it," Hutch said. "It was the day you served corned beef and cabbage."

Laughing, Linda said, "May I have the floor long enough to say I'm glad to know you, Huggy Bear?"

"My pleasure, ma'am." He lifted three menus from a pile on the backbar and handed them around. "You people gonna drink anything?"

"On duty, Huggy," Starsky said.

"Then I'll be back after I take care of some other thirsty customers."

When he came back, Hutch ordered a luncheon of organic food that Angie the chef stocked specially for him and a few other customers who were on health-food diets. Starsky ordered a chile size, and the girl ordered a salad plate. After Huggy Bear put in the orders, Hutch called him over again.

"Any word on that leak yet?" he asked.

"No, but I got a good lead on it. Buddy of mine's married to the girl does housework for the niece of Kester's private secretary. My buddy's got his wife working on the niece to work on her aunt."

"Sounds like a long chain," Starsky said. "Think anything will come of it?"

Huggy Bear shrugged. "You'd be surprised how much can filter down through even longer chains."

He went away to wait on other customers. Starsky said, "Think I better phone the hospital to arrange a few security precautions."

Sliding from his stool, he went over to the phone booth and closed himself inside. After looking up a number, he dialed.

"Southern Memorial," a feminine voice said.

"Room 541, please."

In the middle of the first ring a voice answered, "Jenkins."

"Al Jenkins?" Starsky asked. "The famous cop?"

"Yeah, Starsky," Jenkins said, recognizing his voice. "What's up?"

"What are visiting hours there in the afternoon, Al?"

"Two to three."

"Okay. For today I want you to arrange with the hospital authorities to have the start of the visiting hour delayed until twenty after two for the fifth floor only. Maybe they can let it run until twenty after three. Between two and two-twenty I don't want anyone at all on fifth except patients and hospital personnel. Can you swing that?"

"No problem, Starsk. Visitors have to get tags in the lobby, because only two at a time per patient are allowed. I'm sure the hospital people will cooperate. You moving Mello?"

Mindful of the leak, Starsky simply said, "No, not yet. This has to do with another problem. See you about two, Al."

Instead of returning immediately to the bar, he detoured to the candy machine near the front door.

When he rejoined Hutch and Linda, he was peeling the wrapper off a chocolate bar. The girl looked at it in astonishment.

"You're going to eat that *now?*" she inquired.

"Don't question it," Hutch advised. "You'll get a lecture on how the Chinese eat dessert first, or how it all mixes together in your stomach anyway, or on something equally revolting. You'll be happier if you just pretend you don't notice him chomping on candy two minutes before his lunch is delivered."

Actually it was delivered before he finished the candy bar, so that she was treated to the curious sight of Starsky alternating bites of chocolate with bites of his chile size.

Chapter XX

SHORTLY BEFORE 1:30 P.M. a dark-blue panel truck drove onto the hospital parking lot. This time young Arnie Schultz was driving. Jeremy Tober was in front with him and Max Jefko was in back. It was early enough before the visiting hour started for the lot to be uncrowded. Arnie found a spot directly across from the side door where he could park the truck with its back to the door.

"Perfect," Tober said approvingly as they all got out.

Tober was wearing a suit and necktie, but the other two were in short-sleeved sport shirts. The bottom of Jefko's shirt was hanging out to conceal the gun stuck in his belt, but Arnie's was tucked in because he wasn't armed.

They went in, climbed the stairs to the second floor,

and posted themselves at the window at the end of the hallway overlooking the parking lot. The three of them were still standing there twenty minutes later when the red-and-white Torino pulled onto the lot.

"Okay," Tober said to Arnie. "Get an elevator and hold it for us."

Arnie hurried along the hallway toward the elevators. The other two remained by the window, watching. By that time the parking lot was fairly well filled, as the visiting hour was to start in ten minutes. The Torino had to park at the far end of the lot. Tober and Jefko watched the two men and one woman get out of the car and start their way. Both recognized Detectives Starsky and Hutchinson, even from a distance, but they had to wait until the trio came closer in order to get a good look at the girl with them.

When the three were within seventy-five feet of the side door, Tober said, "Get a good make on her, because Kester will blow his cork if we burn the wrong girl."

"I got it," Jefko said.

Together they walked rapidly along the hall to the elevators. Arnie was holding the one on the right. As they stepped on, Arnie released the hold button, and Tober pressed *B*.

When the elevator door opened in the basement, Tober said to Arnie, "Hold it again," stepped off, and grabbed one of the gurneys. Wheeling it into the car, he said, "Hit the five button."

At the fifth floor Tober wheeled the gurney off the elevator. Jefko got off too, but Arnie stayed on, his finger depressing the hold button.

Looking around, Tober said irritably, "Not now. Let it go."

Arnie stepped off the car, and immediately the door closed behind him as someone on another floor pushed the call button.

Through the open door of the supply room across the hall they could see an orderly standing on their side of the counter while the pudgy attendant piled a stack of sheets. Cursing under his breath, Tober ran the gurney over against the wall on that side of the corridor, out of sight of both men in the supply room. Glancing over at the floor indicator panels, he was relieved to see that both elevators were on upper floors. The three of them waited for the orderly to leave.

The same feminine voice they had heard twice earlier said from a speaker, "Dr. Ferris, please. Paging Dr. Ferris."

"Can't they ever find that guy?" Tober muttered. "Probably got a nurse in some vacant room."

The orderly emerged from the supply room carrying the stack of sheets and turned in the opposite direction, so that his back was to them. Tober immediately pushed the gurney through the door into the supply room. Jefko and Arnie followed him inside. After swinging the gurney around to face back toward the door, Tober took a small cardboard sign with an adhesive backing from his inside pocket and slapped it on the outside of the door. The sign read CLOSED. He closed and locked the door.

The pudgy attendant, both puzzled and a little apprehensive, asked, "What can I do for you gentlemen?"

Tober said, "We need a sheet, surgical cap, mask, set of whites, stethoscope, an orderly's white coat, size medium, and a hospital nightgown, also size medium."

His eyes bugged, the attendant asked, "What for?"

"We're going to play doctor," Tober said, casually producing a .38 automatic and leveling it at the man.

The attendant's astonishment turned to terror. Hurriedly he moved to collect the ordered items and pile them on the counter. Meantime Jefko was standing at the door, peering through the small square window in it at the elevators across the hall. Young Arnie merely stood there, breathing heavily.

When everything was on the counter, Tober walked behind it and said, "Turn around."

The attendant obediently turned his back. The gun

rose and descended on the back of his head. He fell forward like an axed pine tree and lay still.

Jefko announced, "They just got off the elevator."

"Okay, Arnie," Tober said briskly, picking the orderly's white coat from the counter and tossing it to him. "Get this on, and as soon as they're around the corner, get over across the hall and bring up an elevator. Anybody asks you why you're holding it, tell 'em Dr. Ferris told you to."

Coming from behind the counter, he tossed the hospital gown to Jefko and hurriedly began to don the doctor's uniform. After buttoning his white coat, Arnie peered through the small window, then unlocked the door and went out. Jefko, by then in his hospital gown, relocked the door behind him and lay on his back on the gurney. Tober took his gun from his belt and laid it on the gurney next to Jefko's right shoulder. When he finished putting on his doctor's uniform, including the surgical cap and mask, he hung the stethoscope around his neck. Then he covered the prone Jefko up to the chest with the sheet. Jefko draped his left arm across his stomach, outside the sheet, but kept his right, holding his gun, beneath it.

Tober went over to peer out the window. Just as he looked out, the left elevator door opened, Arnie stepped into the car, and pressed the hold button. Tober fixed his gaze on the corner around which the detectives would appear with the daughter of Andrew Mello, and waited.

He said to the man lying on the gurney, "Remember, we want her alive, no matter how many cops we have to burn."

There were different cops on duty in the corridor outside Mello's and his daughter's rooms than there had been early that morning, and neither knew Starsky and Hutch by sight. Both they and Linda had to show their ID's before the guards would pass them into room 541.

The hospital room was rather crowded. In addition to the patient, there was his daughter, the uniformed policewoman who had been serving as her personal bodyguard, Captain Dobey, and the two inside guards. Starsky and Hutch knew both of them.

To the older of the two, a stocky middle-aged man with a slight paunch, Starsky said, "You get the visiting hours changed, Al?"

"Yeah, Starsk. No trouble."

Captain Dobey said to the uniformed policewoman, "You're relieved of duty, Addison. Starsky and Hutch will take over now."

"Yes, sir," she said. "Good-bye and good luck, Miss Mello."

"Thank you for everything," Mello's daughter said.

The policewoman left the room.

The captain turned to Joanne. "You understand that you aren't out of the woods even after you reach Paris? Harry Kester has overseas friends too. Only after your father finishes testifying, not only before the grand jury, but also in superior court at Kester's trial, will you be completely out of danger."

Nodding, she said, "I realize that, Captain."

"So obey the security rules and keep Detective Williams with you at all times. Okay?"

"I will," she assured him. "I'm not anxious to fall into Kester's hands."

Looking at his watch, Dobey said, "It's just two. You better head for the airport."

Joanne kissed her father good-bye. Then she indicated a large suitcase on the floor next to the wall and said to Starsky and Hutch, "That's all the luggage I have."

The detectives exchanged glances inviting each other to do the honors. Starsky said, "Actually both of us ought to have our hands free."

"Of course," Hutch agreed. He said to Captain Dobey, "Guess you're elected to carry the suitcase down to the car, Captain. Starsk and I are on body-guard duty."

The captain was not used to serving as a redcap, but he was too much of a gentleman either to make Joanne Mello carry her own suitcase or to order Detective Williams to carry it. Looking slightly miffed, he picked it up and preceded the others from the room.

Starsky went out next, glanced along the corridor, then gestured to Joanne that it was safe to follow. She paused in the doorway long enough to throw her father a good-bye smile and say, "Get well fast, Dad."

"Sure, honey," he said. "Have a nice flight."

They moved along the hall in procession, Dobey in front carrying the suitcase, Starsky and the Mello girl behind him, and Hutch and Linda bringing up the rear.

Hutch said, "Linda, something's been bugging me."

"What?"

"When it started, we didn't know you were a cop, but you knew we were."

"I thought we settled all that," she said reproachfully.

Hutch made a dismissing gesture. "I'm not talking about the way you suckered us. Just seemed that for a fellow cop, you were running a little scared. That part of the act?"

"Not really. I was scared. You two could have been a couple of stumblebums for all I knew, and we were up against real pros." She grinned. "Hw could I have known you were just a little short of perfect?"

"Right," Hutch said with a pleased expression on his face. "No way you could."

Dobey turned the corner and started toward the elevators fifty feet beyond. As Starsky and Joanne Mello rounded it just behind him, a door on the left beyond the elevators opened and a gurney was pushed out by a white-smocked doctor wearing a surgical cap and mask. The patient on the gurney had one arm outside the sheet, folded across his stomach.

As the gurney neared, Starsky noted that the exposed left arm and wrist of the patient were abnormally thick. Then his gaze riveted on the oversized black-dialed watch strapped to the wrist.

Grabbing Joanne by the shoulders, he spun her around and gave her a shove back around the corner behind them. As a continuation of the same movement his hand swept to the middle of his back, he fell into a crouch as he drew his gun, and yelled, "Hit it!"

Dobey's reaction was instantaneous. Leaving whatever the danger was for Starsky to handle, he concentrated on the safety of Joanne Mello. Dropping the suitcase, he spun and charged at her like a lunging fullback, engulfing her in his arms and plowing back around the corner out of sight. Hutch and Linda appeared from around the corner at the same instant.

The hit men were caught by surprise. They had planned to open fire at point-blank range, and they were still about forty feet from Starsky. The "doctor" jerked his right hand from beneath the sheet, gripping a pistol. The "patient" rolled off the gurney, entangling himself in the sheet, and fell to his knees.

The pseudo-doctor and Starsky fired at the same instant. Hurrying his shot, the hit man's slug missed Starsky to catch Linda in the left upper arm. As she fell to the floor, crying out in pain, Hutch threw his body on top of her and rolled twice with her in his arms to get her around the corner and out of the line of fire.

Starsky's slug caught the hit man in the chest. He fell belly down across the gurney. The other hit man managed to untangle himself from the sheet, rose to a crouch, and began firing his .38 automatic as rapidly as he could, aiming only in the general direction of Starsky. Starsky dropped flat just as he began to fire, and the fusillade of slugs whistled over his head.

Hutch rolled back into view, his gun out and leveled. He squeezed the trigger once, and the fake patient slammed back against the wall, hit high in the chest. The man hung there for a moment, stunned, then dropped his gun and slid slowly to a seated position on the floor.

Captain Dobey slid around the corner in a crouch, gun drawn, but it was all over.

On the elevator young Arnie Schultz released the hold button and hit the one for the first floor. The door closed and the car sank downward. On the way down he stripped off the orderly's coat and dropped it in a corner.

When the elevator door opened at the first floor, he walked hurriedly, but with attempted nonchalance, to the side door and out into the parking lot. Jumping into the stolen panel truck, he drove off.

Chapter XXI

STARSKY AND HUTCH climbed to their feet and cautiously moved forward toward the hit men. The one lying belly down across the gurney still had a gun in his hand. He was making wheezing noises. Starsky and Hutch kicked the gun from his hand, cuffed his wrists together and left him there.

The other man had already dropped his gun, but was still conscious. As Hutch kneeled next to him, he looked up with pain-dulled eyes and pressed both hands to his chest. Hutch picked up his gun, dropped it in his jacket pocket, and clipped cuffs to the man's wrists.

Both detectives and the captain put away their guns. Starsky picked up the gun he had kicked aside and handed it to Dobey. Hutch gave the one he had picked up to the captain, then ran over to kneel next to Linda, who was now sitting up and gripping her

wounded arm. Starsky rounded the corner too. Joanne
Mello, milk-pale, was backed against the wall. From
the far end of the hall the two uniformed policemen,
guns drawn, were approaching.

Waving them back, Starsky yelled, "It's all over! Get
back to your posts!"

Nurses and orderlies were converging from all directions. Looking up at the first nurse on the scene, Hutch
said, "Think you can find a doctor, quick?"

"I think we need more than one," the nurse said,
glancing toward the two wounded men. She hurried
toward the nurses' station.

"Hurt bad?" Hutch asked Linda.

"Of course it hurts, you dummy," she said, trying
not to cry.

"Doctor be here in a minute," he said soothingly. He
glanced down at her legs. She was wearing a skirt and
sweater, and the skirt had climbed up around her hips.
"Hey, for a cop you've got nice legs."

Releasing her grip on the wounded arm, she started
to reach down to tug her skirt back in place, but
stopped when she realized the hand was covered with
blood. Hutch adjusted it for her.

Gripping her arm again, she said weakly, "Thanks,
I think."

Captain Dobey knelt on the other side of the girl,
gently removed her hand from the wounded arm, and
examined the wound. "Much pain?" he asked.

"I can still make that plane to Paris," she said in a
suddenly firm voice.

"Afraid not, honey," he said gently but just as
firmly. "It doesn't look serious, but it's going to take
more than a Band-Aid."

Tears welled in her eyes, and she looked at him
beseechingly. He gave his head a regretful shake.
"We're just too pushed for time. I'll have to replace
you. The tickets in your purse?"

She gave a forlorn nod. "The expense money too."

Her purse was lying on the floor. Picking it up,
Dobey removed the three envelopes and handed them

to Starsky. "I'll have another policewoman meet you at the airport," he said. "Give her these." He hurried off toward the nurses' station to make a phone call.

Looking up at Hutch with a tear running down one cheek, Linda said, "Is it all right for a cop to cry? It's not over the pain, it's over Paris."

"Sure, honey," he said. "Cry all you want."

A doctor came along, politely asked Hutch to get out of the way, and knelt next to the wounded girl. He scissored away the sleeve of her sweater and began putting a temporary bandage on the wound. Meanwhile another doctor was examining the two wounded hit men.

With nothing to do but watch, Starsky and Hutch moved aside. Hutch said to Starsky, "How'd you know it was them?"

"The watch."

"What?" Hutch asked puzzledly.

"The guy pushing the stretcher had on a surgical cap and mask."

"So?"

"So the guy on the stretcher was supposedly either going or coming from surgery, right?"

"Seems logical."

"So the patient was wearing that great big wristwatch. You don't wear a watch in surgery."

Hutch looked impressed. "That's my watch-happy partner."

Linda, listening to the conversation while the doctor wound gauze around her arm, tried to put on a brave front by saying to Hutch, "And you said he was just another pretty face."

"I lied," Hutch said, smiling at her.

Two other gurneys had been wheeled into the area. Linda was lifted onto one, the wounded man seated on the floor was lifted onto the second, and the other wounded man had been turned over on his back on the gurney he already occupied by a couple of orderlies. All three were wheeled onto elevators.

Dobey came hurrying back. "All set," he said.

"Helen Comstock will meet you at the reservation desk a half-hour before flight time. Terry's phoning the airport to change the reservation."

Then he looked at Joanne Mello, who still leaned against the wall, looking pale. "You all right, Miss Mello?"

"Yes," she said, straightening up and getting a grip on herself. "I'm sorry Linda has to miss the trip. I'm going to make it up to her somehow."

"You may miss it yourself if we don't get moving," Dobey said. He picked up the suitcase he had dropped and continued on to the elevators.

After carrying the suitcase to the Torino, Captain Dobey returned to the hospital to check on the conditions of the three wounded people. Starsky and Hutch gave him their handcuff keys so that he could uncuff the two suspects if he wanted to.

During the ride to the airport Starsky kept one eye on the rearview mirror and Hutch kept studying the cars alongside them. Halfway there, Starsky suddenly emitted a bitter chuckle.

"What's funny?" Hutch asked.

"Nothing. Just occurred to me we're getting paranoid about Kester. He can't have guns *everywhere*."

"Don't be too sure," Hutch said. "Did you expect them to pop out of the woodwork at the hospital?"

They reached the airport without incident. Starsky drove along the airport drive slowly, looking for the Air France sign. When he finally spotted it, he turned left onto the parking lot reserved for that line, pulled up alongside the self-service ticket machine, and ripped off a ticket. The barrier, a miniature railroad gate, raised, and he drove on through.

Although the total parking area at Los Angeles International Airport is enormous, the individual parking lots for each airline are not particularly large. Starsky managed to find a slot only one lane in, directly across from the terminal building. As he pulled into the slot, a gray panel truck backed from a space in the first lane, drove down to the end, and made a U-turn into their lane.

This time it was Hutch who sensed the danger. He was just helping Joanne out of the back seat when the panel truck turned into their lane. "Down!" he yelled, shoving her back inside so violently that she sat on the floor with a bump.

Starsky, who was already out of the car and in the act of pocketing the keys, instinctively dove in front of the Torino. Hutch crouched behind the open rear door. The panel truck braked to a halt directly behind the Torino and a silenced automatic made a series of popping sounds that were not nearly as loud as the noise the slugs made as they slammed into the door Hutch was behind.

Starsky popped up, drew a two-handed bead on the man firing the silenced gun, and put a bullet through his head. As the panel truck started to surge on, Hutch fell flat, fired twice from under the car door, and blew out both tires on the near side. The vehicle swerved out of control to the right and crashed into the back of a parked Cadillac.

Starsky ran past Hutch to cover the door on the driver's side of the truck while Hutch was climbing to his feet. By the time Hutch got there, the driver was climbing out with his hands up.

"Don't shoot," he said in a high voice. "I'm not armed."

The man was skinny, not very tall, and no more than twenty-two. Swinging him around, Starsky slammed him face down across the hood of the panel truck. While Starsky was shaking him down, Hutch examined the passenger in the front seat and saw he was dead. Going around back, he jerked open the rear door and peered inside. When he saw nothing there except some blankets and a coil of rope, he put away his gun.

Starsky put away his too, jerked the suspect around to face him, and said, "Okay, Turkey, get up a driver's license."

Producing a wallet, the man fished out a license and handed it over.

"Well, well," Starsky said to Hutch. "Young Jonathan Marrs, the owner of the motorcycle that was so conveniently stolen while he was up in Frisco." He handed the license back and told the man to put it away.

"Not surprised," Hutch said. "The corpse in the front seat is Curly Dobbs, and his left arm's in a sling. Kind of imagine he was the passenger on the back of that motorcycle."

Hutch went to check on Joanne Mello, and found her still cowering on the back floor of the Torino. As he helped the shaken girl from the car, a jeep drove onto the lot and four airport police jumped out with drawn guns.

"What was all that shooting?" the sergeant in charge asked in an authoritative voice.

Starsky and Hutch both showed their ID's. "Kidnap attempt," Hutch told the sergeant. "We have to get this young lady here on the four o'clock flight to Paris." He looked at his watch. "That's in forty-five minutes. Can we leave this mess in your hands and explain it after we see her off?"

"If it was a kidnap attempt, she'll have to stay here to file a complaint," the sergeant said.

"She doesn't want to file a complaint," Hutch said. "Look, Sergeant, it's a matter of top priority that she makes her plane. If she doesn't, the D.A., the chief of police, and our captain are all going to be after the hides of whoever made her miss it. We'll have to refer them to you."

After considering this, the sergeant said, "Okay, but come in to the airport police office as soon as she takes off." He looked at Dippy Marrs. "If she's not going to file a complaint, what do you want this guy held on?"

"Try conspiracy to murder a couple of police officers," Starsky suggested. "Or reckless driving. We're fresh out of cuffs, incidentally. You'll only need one pair. The guy in the front seat is dead."

The sergeant produced a pair of handcuffs. "Hope your truck is insured," he said to Dippy as he cuffed his hands behind him. "The owner of that Cadillac is going to hand you a hell of a bill."

"Ten to one it's stolen," Starsky said. He went over to examine the bullet holes in the door of the Torino. "This thing spends more time in the repair shop than on the street recently," he complained.

"Open the trunk so we can get Miss Mello's suitcase," Hutch said. "Let's get her on that plane before any more Kester guns show up."

As he opened the trunk, Starsky asked his partner the same question Hutch had put to him at the hospital. "How'd you know it was them?"

"The exit arrows pointed straight ahead," Hutch said. "There could be only two reasons for them to pull in the lane where we were. Either they were looking for a parking place, or looking for us. And they had just pulled out of a perfectly good parking place."

Chapter XXII

THEY RAN INTO no further problems. Policewoman Helen Comstock, a buxom blonde of about thirty, was waiting at the reservation desk with a suitcase. Starsky turned over to her the two flight tickets and the expense money. He and Hutch accompanied the women to the loading gate and watched them board the plane. They waited until the plane took off.

It was nearly 5 P.M. before they finished at the office of the airport police. Then they had to drive the handcuffed Dippy Marrs down to Parker Center and book him on conspiracy and for possession of a stolen vehicle. By then it was 6:30, but they found Captain Dobey still in his office. just getting ready to leave.

"How'd it go?" the captain asked as they came into the office.

"Joanne and Officer Comstock are en route to Paris," Hutch said. "But we had another gun battle at the airport."

Dobey removed his hat, hung it up, and went back to sit behind his desk. "Okay, let's have the details," he said.

Hutch gave him a brief but thorough résumé of what had happened. When he finished, Dobey said, "Our leak seems to be getting more efficient all the time. Not a damn soul aside from we three, Coleman, and Detective Williams knew you'd be pulling onto that particular parking lot at the airport at that particular time."

"This office *has* to be bugged," Starsky said.

The captain shook his head. "The bug experts from Intelligence Division went over it."

"They missed the bug," Starsky insisted. "You know none of the five people here this morning ratted. I remember thinking while Linda was signing that voucher that this time there *couldn't* be a—" He came to an abrupt halt.

Dobey and Hutch looked at him curiously. "Why'd you stop?" Hutch asked.

Starsky looked from one to the other with a wondering expression on his face. "We're none of us very bright," he said. "Ever read that classic mystery story about the eavesdropping waiter?"

"What mystery story?" Dobey asked puzzledly.

"I don't remember who wrote it, but there was this group of business associates who always met at the same restaurant and sat at same table. They couldn't figure out how their competitors always guessed what their next move was going to be. The answer was the waiter. They talked freely in front of him because they weren't really aware he was there. A good waiter tends to be invisible. Ever read that story?"

"I hate mystery stories," Hutch said. "Too much like a busman's holiday."

"There's somebody else just as invisible," Starsky said. "Somebody who blends into the background of an office just like a waiter blends into the background of a restaurant. Somebody you take for granted as part of the office equipment, on a par with file cabinets and desks and typewriters."

"Judas Priest!" Dobey said. "Terry Evers!"

"Yeah. You two feel as stupid as I do?"

In a tone of self-disgust the captain said, "I feel stupider. You two only glimpse her once in a while, but I see her around here all day."

"That's why you never thought of her," Starsky pointed out. "She's part of the environment."

Rising, the captain went over to a file cabinet, thumbed through a drawer and drew out a personnel card. Reading from it, he said, "Born March 6, 1948, in Van Nuys. Graduated high school 1966, business college 1969. Passed the civil service exam for civilian steno same year, has worked for the city ever since, but only for the police department the past six months. She's been with public works, city clerk's office, and the fire department. Came here when she passed her secretary's exam. Assigned as my secretary two months ago."

"What's her address?" Hutch asked.

The captain read off an address in the eleven-thousand block of Wilshire Boulevard. "Must be a pretty big apartment building," he said. "She's on the sixteenth floor. Apartment 1608."

"That's in West Los Angeles," Starsky said. "Aren't rents kind of high in that area?"

"Beyond my income," Dobey said.

"She married?" Hutch asked.

Looking at the card again, Dobey shook his head. "No indication here that she ever was. There's boxes for divorced and widowed, but she checked single. So she's not drawing alimony."

"Maybe she lives with her parents," Starsky suggested.

The captain shook his head again. "Card says both parents are dead." He replaced the card, closed the file cabinet drawer, and returned to his desk. "I want her checked out. Tonight."

"We haven't even had dinner," Starsky protested. "And it's pushing seven o'clock."

"The cafeteria's still open," Dobey said without sympathy.

"Okay," Starsky said with a sigh. He looked at Hutch. "Are you going to eat yogurt in front of me again?"

" 'Course not. That's breakfast. I'll probably have liver, if it's on the menu."

Starsky made a face. "Not much better," he muttered to himself.

Dobey said, "Now that you've got me thinking about Terry, I realize the signs were there all along. I remember a couple of times seeing her using that pay phone down the hall and wondering why she didn't use the one on her desk."

"Maybe you ought to have the pay phone tapped," Hutch suggested.

"Hey, good idea," the captain said. "I'll give Intelligence a ring."

Starsky got up and gestured for Hutch to get up too. "If were going to have to work all night, let's grab some grub and get started," he said.

"Hang on a minute," Hutch said. "Captain, how was Linda Williams when you left the hospital?"

"Okay, except for being depressed about missing the trip to Paris. It was just a flesh wound. Should be out in a couple of days."

"What about the two guys Hutch and I shot?" Starsky asked.

"Both listed as serious, but expected to live. They're a couple of known Kester hoods named Max Jefko and Jeremy Tober."

"Hell, we know them," Hutch said to Starsky.

"Not in those outfits, I didn't," Starsky said. "Either one talk, Captain?"

The captain gave him a quizzical look. Starsky grinned. "Dumb question, I guess. Hey, you bring our handcuffs back?"

Opening a desk drawer, Dobey took out the two sets of cuffs and the keys and laid them on the desk. Starsky and Hutch put them away and headed for the door. The captain was dialing a number, presumably Intelligence Division, as they left the office.

It was 8:30 when Starsky and Hutch arrived at the apartment building in West Los Angeles. It was a sleek, modern building of steel and glass surrounded by a manicured lawn edged by a row of tall palms.

As they rode the elevator to the sixteenth floor, Starsky asked, "What do we say to her?"

Hutch said, "We were just passing through the neighborhood and decided to drop in. Nothing strange about a single guy dropping in on an attractive single woman."

"Maybe not. But *two* guys? You don't take a buddy along once you get out of high school."

After considering this, Hutch said, "You're right. Why don't you just go back down to the car?"

The elevator door opened and Hutch got off. Starsky asked, "How long you going to leave me sitting in the car? Maybe she has funny tastes in men, and will invite you to spend the evening."

"Probably will," Hutch said modestly. "But I'll make some kind of excuse."

Someone on another floor pushed the call button then, and the elevator door closed between them. Starsky pushed the button marked *L*.

The car stopped at the sixth floor, and a middle-aged couple got on. The man looked at the control board, saw that the *L* button was lighted, and pushed the one below it marked *G*.

The elevator stopped at the lobby, but on impulse Starsky remained in the car. After a few moments the door closed again and the car descended to the basement garage.

The couple got off and made for a far corner of the garage. Getting off also, Starsky glanced around. Seeing that the support pillars had numbers and directional arrows painted on them to guide tenants to their parking places, he followed the arrows to the space designated for apartment 1608.

In this high-rent district, each tenant had two assigned parking slots. In 1608's space there was a two-year-old Volkswagen and a brand-new cream-color Cadillac.

Either Terry Evers had a visitor, or more money than she earned as a secretary, Starsky thought. Both cars were locked, but with a thin wire picklock, he managed to get into the Cadillac. The car registration in the glove compartment showed that the owner was Terry Evers.

Starsky relocked the car, walked up the exit ramp leading from the garage to Wilshire Boulevard, and down the street to where the Torino was parked. He sat in it and waited. And waited.

Eventually he switched on the dashlight long enough to look at the clock. It registered 9:35. Adding the ten minutes it would have lost since Hutch set it two days ago, he figured it was a quarter to ten.

Then in the rearview mirror he saw Hutch come from the apartment building. A few moments later he slipped into the front seat alongside Starsky.

"I was beginning to think you were going to spend the night," Starsky said.

"I had an invitation. I didn't think it would be chivalrous to sleep with a woman, then arrest her the next day."

"You're all heart," Starsky said sourly. "Learn anything?"

"That she's got about five thousand dollars' worth of stereo equipment, a bar stocked with everything, and an apartment that must cost her six hundred dollars a month."

"She also has a brand-new Cadillac in the basement garage," Starsky said. "Registered in her name."

"Think we need anything else?" Hutch asked.

"I think it would only be gilding the lily," Starsky said. "Let's go home."

Chapter XXIII

IN THE MORNING Starsky again left the Torino in the police department garage for repairs. He and Hutch met Captain Dobey in the latter's office at twenty past eight, ten minutes before Terry Evers was due at work.

"Well?" Dobey asked as the two detectives seated themselves.

"She's living way beyond her means," Hutch said. "High-rent apartment, expensive furnishings, a Cadillac."

"A Cadillac!" the captain said.

"Cream-color job," Starsky said. "Brand new. Did you get Intelligence to tap that pay phone?"

"Uh-huh."

Pulling open his top left desk drawer, he motioned for Starsky and Hutch to come around next to him. Rising to their feet, the two detectives rounded the desk. There was a small cassette-type tape recorder and a separate speaker in the desk drawer. A wire attached to both ran down the left rear leg of the desk to disappear through a tiny hole in the rug.

The captain closed the desk drawer and the detectives returned to their chairs. Hutch asked, "How do you want us to play things?"

"By ear," Dobey said. "Just follow my lead."

The door opened and Terry Evers stuck in her head. " 'Morning, Captain," she said. She nodded to Starsky, gave Hutch a warm smile, and said, " 'Morning, Hutch."

"Hi," Hutch said cordially. Starsky, deciding his nod deserved only a nod in return, gave her one. The captain said, " 'Morning. Want to bring us some coffee?"

"Not for us," Hutch said. "Starsky and I just had breakfast."

"One coffee then," the secretary said agreeably, and closed the door behind her.

"How come you order for me?" Starsky asked Hutch. "Or, rather, unorder."

"You drink too much coffee."

"You eat too much yogurt," Starsky said. "But do I complain?"

"Several times a day," Hutch informed him.

Terry entered carrying a Styrofoam cup and set it on the captain's desk.

Dobey said to Starsky and Hutch, "Okay, we'll move Mello to the safe house in the Valley this afternoon. What's that address again?"

Both detectives momentarily looked blank, but then Starsky grabbed the ball. "Corner of Jefferson and Marshall. What time you want us to move him?"

"Let's make it about two. But this time we're taking no chances at all. Instead of using one of the main elevators, I want you to take him down on the freight elevator behind the nurses' station. You have to go through the station to get to it, but I'll get permission for you to do that from the hospital authorities."

Starsky and Hutch both nodded. Starsky said, "We'll have to use Hutch's Ford, because the Torino's in getting another face-lift."

"Anything else, Captain?" the secretary asked.

"Not now, Terry. Thanks."

The girl left the room, closing the door behind her. After waiting a minute, Hutch got up, cracked open the door and peered into the outer office. He watched a few moments, then closed the door again.

"She just left the office," he said.

Captain Dobey pulled open his desk drawer and threw a switch. Hutch reseated himself, and they all waited. Nothing happened immediately, but then they heard the buzz of a phone ringing, as it sounds on the receiver when you are making a call.

The buzzing stopped and a feminine voice said, "Kester Enterprises."

"Mr. Kester, please," Terry's voice said.

The three officers looked at each other. Dobey said grimly, "She swallowed the bait."

After a short wait, a male voice said, "Yeah?"

"Terry, Mr. Kester. Listen, they're taking Mello to a house in the Valley this afternoon. Corner of Jefferson and Marshall. The captain referred to it as a 'safe' house."

"That means it's a fortress," Kester said glumly. "We'll have to hit him before he gets there. After yesterday's fiasco, I couldn't get anybody to try for him inside the hospital, so we'll have to figure something different. You know the time of the transfer?"

"Two P.M."

"The route they'll be taking?"

"No, I don't know that, but Starsky and Hutch are the cops making the transfer, and they'll be riding in Hutch's car instead of Starsky's red-and-white job. It's a kind of beaten-up Ford sedan a couple of years old. Dull brown color."

"Okay. Anything else?"

"Yes. They'll be taking Mello downstairs by a freight elevator behind the fifth-floor nurses' station instead of by one of the main elevators. The captain said you can only get in it by going through the nurses' station."

There was a long pause as, presumably, Kester thought this over. Presently he said, "I imagine you can get to it in the basement more simply. Maybe we can arrange a small explosion on the elevator. Thanks for calling."

"You know how to repay me," she said lightly. "Good hunting."

They heard a click as Terry hung up.

Switching off the machine, Captain Dobey said wryly, "Guess we made some work for the bomb squad."

"Give 'em a ring," Starsky suggested. "They can stake the place out and catch the bomber in the act."

"It's not that simple. Far as I know, there's no freight elevator where I said. I made that up for Terry's benefit."

"There has to be one somewhere in the building," Hutch said.

"I suppose. Think I better run over to the bomb squad personally to explain this, instead of just phoning."

"She ought to be back at her desk by now," Hutch said. "Want us to move in?"

"May as well."

"That tape recorder work on batteries as well as electric power?"

"Sure. Why?"

"Thought we might as well fancy up the arrest a little. May we borrow it?"

Unplugging the little recorder, the captain handed it across the desk to him. After briefly examining it, Hutch pressed the *rewind* button. When it had rewound all the way, he got to his feet. "Okay, Starsk," he said. "Let's close in."

The two detectives went into the outer office. Terry Evers was now seated at her desk, doing some paperwork. Hutch set the little tape recorder on a table against the wall and switched it to *play*. Then he went over to sit on the edge of the girl's desk and smiled down at her. She smiled back. Starsky moved in front of her desk and smiled at her too. She returned his smile, but not as warmly.

Her smile became slightly fixed when the buzz of

a phone ringing issued from the tape recorder. It turned into an expression of dazed shock when a feminine voice said, "Kester Enterprises," and her own voice replied, "Mr. Kester, please."

Speaking above the sound of the recorder, Hutch said to Starsky, "How can girl on a secretary's salary own a second car, and a new Caddy at that?" He swung his smile back at the girl. "Maybe her folks send her money."

Starsky sat on the other corner of the desk. "No. Remember her personnel card said her folks are dead? This is her only visible means of support."

The girl was trying to listen both to her own conversation on the tape and the two detectives' conversation. Most of her attention was on them.

Hutch said, "She takes in sewing?"

"I don't think so," Starsky said. "No needle holes. Listen, I fix one shirt, my fingers are simply a mess."

Captain Dobey appeared in the doorway of his office. The girl looked at him sickly. Her voice was saying from the tape recorder, "No, I don't know that, but Starsky and Hutch are the cops making the transfer—"

Hutch said, "Maybe she won the Irish Sweepstakes."

Wrenching her gaze from the captain, she looked up at Hutch and said with a mixture of despair and accusation, "You were spying on me last night. How could you do what you did, and then turn me in?"

"What did he do?" Starsky asked with interest.

Captain Dobey stepped on whatever answer she was going to make by saying, "Book her!"

He turned around to re-enter his office. Hutch went over to shut off the tape recorder. Terry took a purse from a desk drawer and unsteadily got to her feet.

"How'd you know?" she asked Hutch in a weary voice.

Hutch shrugged. "Every time somebody moved, you were making the travel arrangements. So we gave your personal life a little attention." He took her elbow to steer her toward the door. "Listen, you're going to need a very expensive lawyer, so if you want to sell the Caddy, cheap—"

She didn't bother to answer.

Down in the felony section they booked her on a conspiracy charge and turned her over to a police-woman who took her to Sybil Brand Institute for Women. Later the district attorney might choose to ask for an indictment on other charges, including receiving bribes, and possibly as accessory to attempted murder and attempted kidnaping. But for the moment the single charge was enough to hold her until the D.A. made his decision.

When they got upstairs again, District Attorney Coleman was in the captain's office, listening to a replay of the tape. Starsky and Hutch seated themselves and waited for the tape to end.

When Dobey switched off the machine, Coleman said with satisfaction, "So that solves the leak." Then he frowned. "How come you never thought of her sooner, Captain?"

"Did you ever read the mystery story about an eavesdropping waiter?" the captain asked. "These businessmen gathered at the same restaurant every day, and sat at the same table. They couldn't figure out how their business rivals always knew their plans in advance. The waiter was listening to everything they said."

Coleman gazed at him blankly. "What's that have to do with your secretary?"

"I don't think I explained it quite right," Dobey said. He looked at Starsky. "Go over that again."

"The point of the story was that nobody notices a waiter, Mr. Coleman," Starsky said. "Unless he's actually serving you, he's invisible. A secretary is too. She blends into the background so thoroughly, you don't really notice her."

Coleman continued to frown. "Obviously you haven't seen my secretary." Then he made a dismissing gesture. "But no matter. The important thing is the leak is stopped. Too bad we can't use this tape against Kester."

"We can't?" Starsky asked.

"You didn't get a court order to tap the phone. Without such an order, you can't legally record a caller's words unless you inform him you're recording and he agrees."

"You mean we can't use it as evidence against Terry, either?" Hutch asked.

"Oh, yes. That's different. There's no law says you can't tap your own phone. And even though it's a public phone, that phone is a police department one. You're entitled to record outgoing calls only, and you can use the recordings in evidence against the caller, but not against the person called."

"Sounds dumb," Starsky said.

Coleman shrugged. "That's the law. But don't worry about Kester getting off, because I have worse things in store for him. Now that Andrew Mello is well enough to move, he's also well enough to appear before the grand jury. Think I'll have him testify tomorrow."

"We'll get him there," Hutch said. "What time?"

"Nine A.M. I'm sure I'll have no difficulty getting an indictment, in which case I'll immediately have the warrant drawn up. Would you two like to serve it?"

Both Starsky and Hutch smiled, but the smiles were a little wolfish.

"We'd love that assignment," Starsky said.

Chapter XXIV

IT WAS ABOUT 9 P.M. when Starsky and Gwendolyn and Hutch and Linda arrived at Huggy Bear's. At that time of night the dinner rush was over and there were two vacant booths and a vacant table to choose from.

Dianne was behind the bar, and Huggy Bear was seated on a stool in front of it. Tonight he was dressed rather conservatively, for him, in plain blue slacks and a maroon-and-white-striped sport shirt.

There were waiters on duty, but Huggy Bear often personally took care of special customers. When he saw the two couples come in, he rose to go meet them. In a rather depressed voice he asked, "Booth or table?"

"Booth," Starsky said. "Sounds like you're dragging, man. What's hurting you?"

"Life," Huggy Bear said gloomily.

He led the way to one of the vacant booths. The girls slid in next to the wall, Linda favoring her left arm. It wasn't in a sling, and the bandage didn't show because she was wearing her long-sleeved white pantsuit again, but she had obvious difficulty moving it.

As Starsky and Hutch seated themselves, Huggy Bear said to Starsky in the same depressed voice, "Cindy phoned for you."

The red-headed Gwendolyn glared at Starsky. He said, "My cleaning lady?"

Huggy Bear, who was always fast on the uptake, caught the redhead's expression and said quickly, "Yeah. She phoned that she can't clean your place Wednesday."

Starsky and Hutch spoke together. Starsky said, "She comes on Tuesday." Hutch said, "She comes on Monday."

"Whatever," Huggy Bear said in an equable tone. "Anyway, she won't be there. What you all want to drink?"

They all ordered beer. When the black man moved away, the red-headed girl said to Linda, "Do you know this Cindy?"

Linda shook her head. "I'm from San Francisco."

Anxious to change the subject, Starsky asked, "When do you have to go back?"

"I'm on ten days' sick leave. But I don't go back even then. I'm flying to Paris."

"Paris!" Gwendolyn said enviously, forgetting all about Cindy.

Hutch said to Starsky, "Andrew Mello's picking up the tab. Partly for selfish reasons, I think. He feels better about having two bodyguards with his daughter."

"You may have a long vacation," Starsky said to Linda. "Kester's trial could take months."

Hutch said, "But Andrew Mello's going to be the first witness, and once his testimony's in the record, both he and Joanne are safe. There'd be no point in Kester pulling anything after that, because it couldn't help him." He turned to Linda. "My guess is you'll have about a month."

"A month in Paris in the summertime," Gwendolyn said wistfully. "I'd settle for that."

Huggy Bear brought over four beers. Setting them down, he said, "Could I see you guys private for a minute?"

Gwendolyn immediately looked suspicious. Starsky asked, "About what?"

"Cop business."

"Oh, you can talk in front of the girls," Starsky said. "Linda's a fellow cop, and Gwen doesn't understand any conversation unless it's about sex."

The redhead jammed her elbow into his ribs hard enough to make him wince.

Huggy Bear shrugged. "I got that dope you asked me for. Kester's secretary is a woman named Eleanor Carson. She told her niece this, her niece told my buddy's wife, and his wife told him. Remember that chain we talked about?"

"Told him what?" Hutch asked.

"Kester has a mysterious woman contact who feeds him info. Usually by phone, but once she came to the office. The secretary doesn't know who she is, but her first name's Terry, she's blond, good-looking, and about twenty-eight or twenty-nine."

Starsky and Hutch looked at each other. "Terrific!" Starsky said.

Hutch said, "Don't you read the papers, Huggy?"

"Sure I read the papers," Huggy Bear said defensively.

"Well, it was on the front page two days ago that Captain Dobey's secretary, Terry Evers, was arrested for feeding dope to Kester."

"Oh." Huggy Bear thought about this for a minute, then shrugged. "I ain't been readin' lately, 'cause I been too downcast."

"We noticed," Starsky said. "Why don't you pull up a chair and tell us about it?"

"Wait till I get a beer," Huggy Bear said.

He went over to the bar, returned with a draft beer, drew a chair away from the vacant table, and sat down on the edge of the booth.

After taking a sip of his beer, he said, "Remember I introduced you guys to little Miss Treasure Chest?"

"Yeah," Hutch said. "You had it rigged to win the grand prize. So how come you're not in the Bahamas?"

Huggy Bear emitted a sigh. "That's a long, sad story. I got clear to the finals." He took another sip of beer.

"Then what happened?" Starsky asked. "Don't keep us in suspense."

"I was asked who was the sixteenth president of the United States. I said Lincoln. The speed of light? I answered precisely one hundred and eighty-six thousand miles a second. Then the big one, for the trip to the Bahamas."

"And some other stuff too, wasn't it?" Hutch asked.

The black man gave a sad nod. "And the TV set, and the freezer full of buffalo meat." He sighed again.

"Will you get to it?" Starsky said impatiently. "What happened!"

"Well, I got so rattled, I couldn't think. My skull started to spin, and little Miss Treasure Chest was grinnin' at me, and the crowd was yellin', and I guess I didn't hear the question right."

"What was the question?" Hutch asked.

"Who was the greatest money-making horse of all time?"

"Man o' War," Starsky said. "Everybody knows that. What did you say?"

"Marie Antoinette."

"Marie Antoinette!" Hutch said. "The greatest money-making horse of all time was Marie Antoinette!"

"I didn't think they said horse," Huggy Bear said sadly.

Gwendolyn emitted a giggle, then everyone else at the table laughed.

"See?" the redhead said to Starsky. "I'm not as dumb as you think. I was the first one to get it."

"That's because it was about sex," he told her. She jabbed her elbow into his ribs again.

"Hey," he protested. "You're going to dig a permanent dent in my side."

"Not if you start being nice to me," she said crossly.

Starsky turned back to Huggy Bear. "Your trouble, man, is you been on the street too long. What happened with Miss Treasure Chest?"

"Oh, she got to the Bahamas, all right. With some other dude."

Starsky shook his head sympathetically. "You've had a bad time, man."

"Pre-cisely. But you guys been havin' it kind of

tough recently too, what with gettin' shot at so much
and all."

"That's part of the game," Starsky said. "Worst
thing that happened was losing my watch." He had a
sudden thought. "Hey," he said to Hutch. "Didn't that
cabbie pick up his heap today?"

"Yeah," Hutch said, a trifle uneasily.

"He didn't turn in my watch!" Starsky said in an
accusing voice. "I can tell it by your expression."

Hutch held up a hand, palm out. "Hold it, hold it.
He did turn in your watch."

"So where is it?"

"Well, there were complications."

"It's broken!" Starsky said.

Hutch shook his head. "Worse than that. The claims
officer found it listed on the hot sheet, and the owner
has been contacted."

Starsky looked stunned. Slowly he turned to look
at Huggy Bear. "You sold me a hot watch!"

Huggy Bear also raised a hand, palm out. "I swear,
man, it was cold when I touched it."

"You sold me a hot watch!" Starsky repeated in a
louder voice.

"I told you how I got it," Huggy Bear said placat-
ingly. "My buddy give it to me to pay off a debt. Said
it was clean. Think he said he won it in a poker
game."

"You sold me a hot watch!" Starsky said even more
loudly.

Glancing around apprehensively, Huggy Bear said,
"Shh—you gonna have all the customers lookin' this
way. It wasn't on purpose, man. You know I'm not no
fence."

Starsky glared at him. Huggy threw an appealing
look at Hutch. Hutch gave a noncommittal shrug indicating he was staying out of it.

Starsky started to open his mouth again. Holding up
his hand and rising to his feet, Huggy Bear said, "Hold
it. Just hang on one little minute."

He went over to the bar, around behind it, and

rang up *no sale* on the cash register. Lifting out the coin receiver, he removed some bills from beneath it, counted them, laid some on the backbar, and put the rest back in the register. Picking up the pile on the backbar, he returned to the table and handed the money to Starsky.

"Three hundred sixty dollars," he said. "Anyone ever tell you you was pushy?"